D0060350

Ellis Peters has gained universal acclaim for her crime
novels, and in particular for *The Chronicles of Brother
Cadfael*, now into their eighteenth volume.

The Will and the Deed

Ellis Peters

HEADLINE

First published in 1960
by William Collins Sons & Co Ltd

Reprinted in this edition in 1991
by HEADLINE BOOK PUBLISHING

10 9 8 7

The title and the chapter headings are taken from Hugo von
Hofmannsthal's libretto of Richard Strauss's opera, *Der
Rosenkavalier*, in the English version by Alfred Kalisch.

ISBN 0 7472 3570 8

Typeset by Medcalf Type Ltd, Bicester, Oxon.
Printed and bound in Great Britain by
Cox & Wyman Ltd, Reading, Berkshire

HEADLINE BOOK PUBLISHING
A Division of Hodder Headline PLC
338 Euston Road
London NW1 3BH

CONTENTS

CHAPTER I

Let us then lightly meet our fate.
Light must we be,
With spirits light and grasp light-fingered
Hold all our pleasures – hold them and
*   leave them.*

Act 1

The patient, if that was the just word for a cantankerous old woman who was spending her final days on earth in creating chaos all round her, opened her eyes for the last time upon the heavy splendours of her hotel bedroom towards evening, and saw the circle of intent faces stooped over her, agitated even in stillness, like the fantastic decoration of a baroque ceiling. All day they had come and gone like insubstantial wraiths troubling her dreams, but now she saw them clearly, and heard their first murmurs not with the frenzied uneasiness of disorientation, but coolly and intelligently, with the physical ear. No more fever now, only this disinclination ever to move again.

She knew that she was about to die. She would do that, as she had always done everything, with style. If the greatest diva of her generation did not know how to make an exit, who did?

1

They were all there, Miranda red-eyed and amorphous in the folds of her handkerchief, trying to push the boy forward into a front place by the bedside, and the boy hanging stubbornly back, frowning and sulky as usual, but with a kind of awed fascination in his eyes. He had no close experience of death as yet. The doctor was sitting by the bed, his fingers on her pulse, with Trevor leaning over one shoulder and young Neil Everard over the other; and Susan, withdrawn and silent, stood back from them all, half-hidden by the massive carved post of the bed, markedly separating herself from their mourning rights and their expectations.

There was one more face, the only one Antonia wanted to see now. Richard was close beside her, he must have stayed by her bed all the time she had slept that long, hot, unquiet sleep. He leaned forward when he saw that her eyes were open, and the subdued light gleamed on his bald head, and painted gross shadows into all his wrinkles. He was old, too, he was very old. It was a long time since he'd sung opposite her for the last time, the best, the lustiest, the most irrepressible Baron Ochs ever seen on any stage. In his youth he had been the handsomest Don Giovanni, too, slender and gallant. How few operatic Dons can boast really good legs!

'Send them away, Dick.' The threadlike voice was quite clear and still authoritative, though it seemed to come from a great distance. 'I want to talk to you. The rest of you get out. I'm not going yet, I'm not ready.'

If Antonia was not ready to depart, death himself would hardly have the temerity to try and hustle her. Richard Hellier met Dr Randall's eye in silent enquiry, and received a nod which he perfectly understood. 'Why not?' said the resigned glance. 'She's going soon in any case, let her talk.'

'I'll be in the next room with Everard,' he said aloud, and led the way out, marshalling them after him. They grudged going, some of them. Miranda bridled like the horse she so much resembled. These country gentlewomen should never shed tears, even horses would do it more becomingly. However, she went, with some hopeful backward glances in case she was recalled. The boy was glad to go, he knew he would not be wanted at the end. What could Antonia Byrne, dying at seventy-six, want with his twenty-five years and sparse experience? This was one performance for which she needed no accompanist.

It was blessedly quiet in the room now, and for a while she was quiet, too, her hand in Richard's hand on the dark-red silk of the coverlet. The curtains were not yet drawn, and there was still light enough outside to show her the bare branch of a tree shivering in the frost, and one filigree spire of the Votivkirche white against the dull leaden grey of the sky.

'Would you believe it, the first time she came here with me Miranda must have sent away at least a dozen postcards of that place, under the impression that it was St Stephen's.'

'It's what I should expect of her,' said Richard. 'I expect she still thinks the plump lady on the Burg Ring is Queen Victoria.'

She laughed. Her laugh had been famous once, it was a travesty now. The slack cords of the pale old neck tightened and jerked painfully above the foam

3

of lace and brushed nylon, the fallen cheeks
twitched, their high, gaunt bones stained with small
discs of scarlet. The gentian blue of her eyes had
faded to a livid grey, and her scalp shone through
her thinning silver-white hair. All the gallant erection
of her ageing elegance had crumbled between
December's fingers like thawing snow. She saw how
he studied her, and smiled maliciously.

'Am I still beautiful, Dick?'

'I stopped telling you you were beautiful when we
were both in the forties,' said Richard. 'You stopped
enjoying it. It was always a lie in any case. What you
had wasn't beauty.'

'But what I had is gone – whatever it was.' She
watched his face, and it looked as it had looked when
she had told him she was coming out of retirement
and returning to the concert stage. He had not tried
to dissuade her, but she had felt his disapproval and
disquiet with every mile of every journey away from
him. 'I should never have done it, should I?'

'No, you shouldn't. Why did you? You didn't need
the money. I'm sure you didn't need the adulation.'

'I was bored,' she said in a dry whisper, still
smiling. 'Being old, being seemly, being sensible –
I was no good at those things. I didn't know when
I retired how dull it was going to be staying on a
pedestal. If falling off it was the only way to get
down, I'm glad I fell. Now boredom isn't going to be
a problem any more. I'm dying, Dick.'

He knew it, and he did not argue. All he said was:
'I shan't be long after you. Leave me a Boy Scout sign
here and there.'

'I've got something for you. Something to
remember me by. I want to give it to you now.' She

would have liked to press his hand, but her own had no strength. 'In the bottom drawer of that cabinet – I want you to take it now.'

To please her he crossed to the elaborate rococo cabinet, and stooped to open the drawer. Behind him the rustling whisper, clear and faint, said: 'Everything else is taken care of. I made a new will, and young Everard will see to everything. A nice boy. Efficient, too. But he'll never make the lawyer his father was. His heart isn't in it. The box under my writing case, Dick – you see it?'

'Yes, I have it.'

'The case is inside it.'

He knew what it was. He came back to the bed with it in his hands, and stood smiling at her over it. No one else, in all her long and brilliant career of triumphs and gallantries, had ever smiled at her like that. She had had three husbands, and none of them had been Richard, and at least seven lovers, and none of those had been Richard, either; he was something apart and permanent, outlasting them all. She would never have jeopardised their relationship by marrying him.

'You'll keep them safe, won't you? Put them away now, and sit by me. I always wanted you to have them. Nobody but you knows how much they meant to me.'

'I'll keep them safe,' he said.

'To remember me by,' she said again, and smiled.

'You know I shall never forget.'

He slid the leather case into his briefcase, which lay upon the table by the window, and turned the key upon it. The tower of the Votivkirche had faded from sugary white to leaden grey, and withdrawn

5

into the falling dusk. Her voice was failing with the light and chilling with the onset of frost.

'Shall I call them back?'

'No. Why?' She was content as she was. What could they do for her but disturb her? 'Dick, do you remember that hundredth performance?' Her thread of a voice drifted into silence. He remembered everything, his Ochs to her Marschallin, his Almaviva to her Countess, even, once, his Papageno to her Astrofiammante. Why had he failed to appreciate himself in that difficult and lovely part? No one else had ever graced it as he did.

'You mustn't worry, Dick – about the funeral. I've told young Everard – he'll arrange it. I want to be buried here – at least in the same city as Mozart. Though they didn't deserve him – it should have been Prague—'

'Poetic justice,' said Richard, holding both her motionless hands in his, 'they lost him.'

'If they forget where they've put me, too,' she whispered complacently, 'I shan't mind, I shall be in good company.'

'You?' said Richard, smiling. 'I know you better than that. You'll be coming back to read the obituaries.' He saw the last wild gleam in her eyes, and the faint flash of a smile that hardly stirred her features, and then a sudden convulsion of life seized her and she was laughing aloud, and some recovered fire from her youth cast a miraculous bloom upon her aged, sick, shrunken face and made her wonderful again. 'And throwing tantrums if the flowers aren't fine enough,' he pursued. 'And wanting Everard to sue some columnist or other for getting his facts wrong about the affair with Carl Ludwig Rupprecht the Third—'

The breath stopped in her throat, the laughter rattled suddenly off-key, and halted in a deep, indrawn gasp. He sprang to his feet, bending over her with his palms framing her face, calling her softly by name.

The others came crowding in and converged upon her bed. The doctor leaned over her from one side, the young solicitor from the other. Her lips moved, forming soundless words, but the faded eyes were no longer conscious even of looming shapes, even of light.

'—for Richard—to remember me by—'

The curves of laughter grew fixed and still upon her face. She died laughing.

CHAPTER II

*What curious adventures may befall a man
– Not all are to my taste. Here one is far
too much the sport of fate.*

Act 2

The charter aircraft took off from Schwechat in the afternoon of December the 23rd, in light, still frost, under a ceiling of cloud so thin that the hard, silvery-grey sky shone through it, and by night there would almost certainly be a clear heaven and stars. But by then, thought Susan Conroy, they would be in London, and the whole distressful business would be over. There would be a quiet Christmas with the family for her instead of a strenuous round of theatres and parties in Mrs Byrne's train and the murky pavements of London instead of the glittering cold and sparkling air of Vienna; and after the festival, the sobering business of finding another job. She could hardly expect another Antonia; the most she dared hope for would be, perhaps, a minor novelist or a literary agent, preferable at any rate to the finicky old solicitor who had been her first boss.

Not all solicitors, however, are sixty-eight, bald and old-maidish in their ways. She made a careful sidelong examination of Neil Everard, reclining in the seat beside her. Thirty was more his mark, and within an inch either way of six feet, with a shock of reddish-brown hair, and shoulders like a Rugby player. His features were strongly marked, and the look of severe gravity they had worn ever since he arrived in Vienna sat uneasily upon them. She felt that almost anything, a sudden, unexpected incident, one flash of temper among his ill-assorted companions, might crack the façade and let out a totally different and infinitely more attractive young man.

She was well aware that he had slid unobtrusively into this rear seat in order to separate himself as widely as possible from Miranda Quayne and her son, and was now leaning cautiously out into the gangway to reassure himself that there was no risk of the lady attacking him even across the two empty seats between. And certainly she had looked round for him two or three times, vexed that he had not come forward to take the seat opposite, beside Richard Hellier, as she had expected him to do; but Laurence had seated himself squarely beside her, hemming her in, and the black-toqued head, redolent of family mourning, revolved in vain.

'Relax!' said Susan. 'Her gentility won't let her shout at you from there. You're safe until Zurich.'

She had been wanting to make him jump like that ever since the funeral. He was the only one with whom she felt any affinity, or could share a single thought. Richard was remote from them all, withdrawn so far into his memories and his loss that it would have been impious to try to follow him. Dr Randall and Trevor Mason, both old friends of Antonia and proud of their long association with her, were held together in a feverish tension by their mutual jealousy, and like angry children outbidding each other swapped endless stories of their intimacy with the old goddess. Trevor held one ace, for as her business manager he had been with her throughout this last long concert tour, whereas the doctor had merely been summoned in haste after her collapse, along with her solicitor. But as the doctor pointed out, there were perfectly adequate medical men in Vienna, if she had wanted nothing more than competent treatment, and Richard, beyond question her oldest and most intimate friend, had been sent for at the same time, and flown in by the same charter plane. The odious Quayne pair, greedy and anxious, had their eyes fixed on the quarter-million or so Antonia was said to be worth, and could hardly keep their mouths from watering as they uttered their pious tributes to the dead kinswoman who had led them such a dog's life. Only Neil Everard stood apart, like Susan, from the ruthless scramble for the old woman's incalculable favour.

'Well, well!' said Neil, startled out of his gravity. 'She was right, you're not as demure as you look.' It was nice to find that he could produce such an unaffected grin.

'She? Miranda? I can hear her saying it!'

'Mrs Byrne. And it sounded quite different from what you're hearing. She liked you. ''She doesn't kowtow to me,'' is how she put it.'

Susan's eyebrows went up. 'You're telling me she didn't like being kowtowed to?'

'Maybe she did, I don't know. I'd seen her only two or three times before, it was always my father who dealt with her affairs, until he died, last year. My uncle didn't fancy a long trip just at Christmas, so I came in for the job whether I liked it or not. Maybe she did enjoy having people jump when she ordered, but if she did she despised them for doing it. I should say she needed you as a corrective to Miranda. My God,' he said, keeping his voice low, for it had a carrying quality of which, as a solicitor, he had good reason to be wary, 'if I hear "as her only close relatives" just once more!'

'You surely will,' said Susan with sympathy, 'unless you can manage to keep out of range from here to London, and that's going to take some doing.'

'Though to be absolutely fair,' added Neil honestly, after a moment's thought, 'I've never actually heard the son say that, or anything in the same line, for that matter.'

'Why should he, when she's there to do it for him? But they're tarred with the same brush, that pair,' said Susan, with supreme confidence in her own judgment. 'Still, I suppose after being a poor relation for so long, it must be a little demoralising to feel a quarter of a million practically in your hands, and not to be able to get at it. Why didn't you do what they all wanted, read the will immediately after the funeral, and get it over?'

It was a tactless as well as an unnecessary question, she realised it as soon as it was out of her lips. He had insisted on deferring the occasion until their arrival in London because he was the junior partner, and the important clients' affairs were in his uncle's hands, not in his. But he was hardly likely to admit that he had simply been acting under orders. He had withdrawn perceptibly and was threatening to put on his official face again. 'I'm sorry, I can't discuss it.'

'No, of course not, I'm sorry, it wasn't a serious

enquiry.' She shot him a sidelong glance, and smiled at the reserve in his eyes. 'Don't worry, I cherish no expectations whatever. I'd been with Mrs Byrne just over a year, and we got on quite well, but there was no affectionate relationship, and anything she owed me was handsomely paid while she was alive. I promise I won't try to pump you. It's no concern of mine what she's chosen to do with her money.'

She had, as a matter of fact, been quite fond of the old woman, but she was not going to confess to any such weakness. The air was already heavy with other people's professions of devotion and grief.

'You're quite sure she had plenty to leave,' said Neil; but he relaxed again, and sat back beside her with a slightly wry grin.

'It seems to be taken for granted. She must have made a fortune in her younger days, and I know how shrewdly she handled it when she had it. Even discounting,' said Susan with a smile, 'some of the wilder legends. Since we've been in Vienna I've heard half the scandalous reminiscences of the operatic stage from 1910 to 1940, and she seems to have been involved in most of them.'

'Or she liked to pretend she was,' said Neil sceptically.

'She liked it, all right. But some of the stories came from women who would have been only too glad to pinch the lead from her if they could. And did you ever see photographs of her in her prime? She was lovely. As beautiful and fresh as a girl, and as imperial as the women she specialised in. I can see why nobody could touch her as the Marschallin. And I can really believe her private life was the procession of blue-blooded lovers they say it was.

The biggest sensation seems to have been during the First World War, when one of those independent archdukes who were still hanging on to precarious little German principalities went completely overboard for her, and is supposed to have smuggled his family's ancestral diamonds abroad and given them to her. He refused to go back home, and they deprived him of his rights and titles, and he died in exile, leaving Antonia in possession of about two hundred and fifty thousand pounds' worth of crown regalia. Or so they say!'

'Oh, the Treplenburg-Feldstein affair, that old chestnut,' said Neil disdainfully. 'I thought that was forgotten. I remember picking it up from somewhere years ago, and my old man knocking it decidedly on the head. Do they still believe in it?'

'Carl Ludwig was kicked out, that's certain. He died in Nice.'

'So did many another of the wilting royalties who're supposed to have had affairs with Antonia. But I'll believe in the diamonds when I see them. I suppose they'll be digging up all those old scandals now that she's dead.'

'Sunday newspaper stuff? Miranda won't like that.'

'It won't poison the money for her,' said Neil cynically. 'She'll be able to convince herself it's her duty to take it.'

'Are you giving me advance information, after all?'

'No, just a general observation.' He laughed, meeting her eye. 'How on earth did a sister of Antonia's come to have such a respectable daughter? Even by a gentleman farmer, God help us! A rank bad one, by the way. He failed. And then she had to marry another of the same breed! Some women never learn.'

Susan drew breath upon a sudden grudging instinct of sympathy for Mrs Quayne. 'No wonder she attached self and son to Mrs Byrne like leeches, and determined to stick it out to the bitter end.'

' "As her only relatives," ' murmured Neil, and shut a hand warningly on her arm as she let out an irrepressible giggle. 'Sssh, I see the black veil twitching.'

Miranda's mourning was indeed of a ceremonious completeness. It had made Susan reflect, as they climbed aboard, that by rights the plane ought to have black plumes mounted above the nose, and crepe streamers trailing from the tail. She was opening her mouth to say so, in a conspiratorial whisper, when she uttered a loud gasp instead, and clutched at the arms of her seat with both hands, for its comfortable support had just dropped from under her. She had hardly noticed how their placid progress had been shaken, in the last ten minutes, by little lurches and steadyings and checks. Here came the first abrupt drop, and the equally unpleasant recovery, saluted by several startled gulps.

'My God, that was sharp!' Neil kept his steadying hold upon her arm, and leaned across her to peer out of the window at the sky where dusk and stars should just have been replacing the clearing film of cloud; but the cloud had thickened and folded in on their passage in convolutions of leaden grey, and the gathering darkness had come more abruptly than it should have done, and was full of turbid movement. 'Weather's changing. Looks like snow, and big snow, too. It's blown up suddenly.'

15

'Whereabouts are we? Do you know?'

'Well past Munich. Should be only half an hour or so to Zurich. May be a bit longer on the journey if we're going to be up against head winds, though. Are you all right?'

'I can take it, unless it gets very bad.' She felt the plane lurch from under her again, and rock and shudder as it came up, and suddenly the warning sign above the cabin door flashed. 'Looks as if he thinks we're in for it, we're being told to buckle ourselves in.'

They groped for their seat belts, and were tossed about so maliciously for a few minutes that they had difficulty in bringing the links together. By the time Susan had the webbing drawn tight, and her weight braced back in the seat against the next plunge, there was sweat dewing her forehead, and she was breathing with the unnatural, measured caution of incipient airsickness. She caught herself at it, and closed her eyes; by now she knew all the simpler aids to relaxation, but they didn't always work. The next moment the slashing of whips across the window close to her face made her open her eyes again quickly. All that was to be seen of the outer world was a dull-grey, whirling darkness that streamed in diagonal lines down the window, first in flakes of melting snow, then in engraved lines of ice. All the voices had fallen silent now. Everyone gripped at the firmest support he could find, and rode the paroxysms as best he could. Even Miranda was silenced.

They seemed to be flying into a strong northwest wind, and a very large and highly charged concentration of cloud. And they must be already over mountain country. Those few degrees' rise in the temperature were going to cost them a nasty passage into Zurich, and maybe a long one, too.

After perhaps a quarter of an hour of hanging on grimly and going where they were thrown there was a lull, or what seemed to them a lull after all they had suffered. Susan opened her eyes cautiously, and unclamped her jaw. Neil was unbuckling his belt. He caught her eye on him, and gave her a somewhat pallid smile of reassurance. 'I'm going in to speak to McHugh, see how things are going.' It was the first intimation she had had that there might be something seriously wrong; unasked reassurances often have the effect of revealing the starting seams of security. She watched his lurching progress up the aisle with anxious eyes. The doctor, on whose tough, desiccated body this violent motion seemed to have little effect, spoke to him as he passed. Miranda stretched out an arm across her son to pluck at his coat, but he saw it in time and eluded her clutch. The narrow metal door opened and sucked him in.

The motion had become violent again by the time he reappeared, and no one had a hand to spare for grabbing at him. The rolling luggage rack had tossed down coats and scarves and small bags upon the heaving bodies beneath, and the windows were opaque with compressed ice. They anchored themselves grimly by whatever afforded a nail-hold, and waited for it to end; there was nothing else for them to do.

Neil held himself upright by the backs of the rocking seats, and yelled above the confusion: 'Keep your belts fastened and no smoking! Sorry about this! Hope we'll make Zurich inside half an hour, but nobody expected this change of wind. Caught the met. offices on the hop. Taken us a bit off course, he says.'

Off course – a northwest gale – southeastwards off course, thought Susan, seeing the map of Europe within her tightly closed eyelids. Farther into the mountains of the northern Tyrol, or that little tongue of Germany that probes down towards the Arlberg. She thought of the knife edges of alpine rock invisible in thickly falling snow, and stopped feeling airsick, having worse things on her mind.

Dimly she heard Miranda's voice for a second, shrill with indignation: 'Disgraceful! What's the use of having meteorological offices? Ought to do better than this—' Then there were minutes of comparative calm, in which she was aware of Neil's weight dropping back into the seat beside her, and comparative silence but for the wind and the lashing of the snow, so that for the first time she caught the strange note of the engine, with that intermittent cough in it.

'All right?'

'Yes, thanks, I'm all right.'

'Good girl!' His voice was low; he leaned closer so that she should not fail to hear him. 'I'm going to move over across the gangway. Don't worry, I'll be keeping an eye on you if anything happens.'

She opened her eyes long enough to take stock of the seat he indicated, and observed that it was beside the emergency door. 'We're in trouble, aren't we? What's he going to do, try and put us down?' Her voice was quite composed. When it came to the point there was no sense whatever in being anything but calm; it didn't mean she wasn't frightened.

18

'Nothing else for it. One engine's packed up on ·him, and he'd have the devil's own job to get us far on the other in this.'

'Does he even know where we are?'

'Somewhere over the Bregenzer Wald, he reckons, not all that far off course. But he says we'd never make Zurich.'

She thought of the rocky outlines of the Vorarlberg, and understood; as well try to land an aircraft on the top of a steeple. 'What does he reckon the chances at?'

'Didn't ask him. I figure they'll be higher if we all leave him alone. Hang on tight, and be ready to move quickly if we do get down intact.'

Gradually they were losing speed and height, she could feel the changes in her ears. The spasmodic note of the engine was louder and more ominous in the moments of relative quietness. Sometimes they seemed almost to hover, and the abrupt downward plunges came more horribly after these lulls. Sometimes the wind caught them broadside and rolled them dizzily, and sometimes met and brought them to a shuddering check from which they recovered groggily, like a sick animal. They could see nothing of the outside world now, the windows were sealed. How much could the pilot see? Once, as they groped their cautious way downwards, feeling for the right trends in the wind channelled and goaded by the mountains, he found a break in the murk just in time, and lifted them clear of a rock wall against which they would have smashed themselves like a gnat hitting a windscreen. Then even more gingerly down again, feeling outwards with quivering senses, and knowing that only luck, not knowledge or skill alone, was ever going to get them safely out of this.

When it came it was brief, and curiously anti-climactic; terrifying, but gone before she had time to experience it fully. Among the heights of the Vorarlberg there are large and comparatively tranquil meadows, and villages within reach of them. The one McHugh found was ample, but dangerously exposed, and he had trouble getting round into the wind, and lost more way then he would have liked, so that there was a horrible moment when the gale brought him up almost standing, and threatened to overturn the aircraft and drop it belly-up into the snow. All they knew of it in the passenger cabin was the sudden tense, shuddering stillness, the sidelong heave of the wind, and then the forward plunge that brought them out of danger. Twenty seconds later they ploughed almost gently into the snow, nose-down.

They were flung headlong left and right, the belts dragging at them agonisingly. The plane heeled once and righted itself, emptying the left-hand rack over their helpless bruised bodies. A series of sickening, grinding lurches, bumping deep into the drifts, the nose bowed and the tail rose a little, and swung uneasily up and down. Then, miraculously, everything was still. The engine had stopped. They could hear the howling of the wind and the steady, malevolent slashing of the snow; the outer world was still there. They were alive.

The pilot came hurtling through the door from his cabin like a gust of wind, capless, streaked with sweat, dragging on his coat as he came. He plunged between the chaos of bodies and bags and magazines, and the ghastly debris of airsickness, towards the emergency door, waving an arm at Neil as he came.

'Open her up! Come on, everybody, out of here, bloody quick! Steady, don't shift the weight back too suddenly.'

He was a big young fellow, and his own weight had been enough to transfer the plane's precarious centre of gravity. The swinging tail settled downwards gently, and stayed down. He felt its solidity, and stamped the settling weight cautiously lower into the encasing snow.

The lever of the emergency door had yielded to Neil's thrust, a narrow oblong of night loomed open before them, and snow whirled in and spattered their faces, thick, soft snow, the kind that seals up whole valleys behind thirty-foot drifts, and when the thaw comes too quickly brings down mountainsides with it.

'You and you!' roared the pilot, still indisputably in command of his aircraft and all who breathed in it, and he reached a great hand for Laurence Quayne's shoulder and dragged him forward from his mother's quivering embrace. 'You're the youngest and heftiest. Get on down there and field this lot. Go on, drop! What are you waiting for, the bloody tank to blow?'

They heard the voice of authority and obeyed it. Surprisingly, Laurence was the first to go. He leaned out from the doorway, took a very brief glance below, and jumped. They heard a muffled shout from the darkness, and then Neil went after him. McHugh cast one glittering glance round his remaining charges, pallid, unkempt, green with shock and sickness. The doctor was small, but tough, intact and already known to him.

'Give me a hand with the women, sir,' he said

briefly, and drew Miranda between them into the doorway. There was a certain toughness about Miranda, too. She made not a sound, and wasted no time in hesitation. When they told her to drop, she dropped. Only when she found herself floundering in three feet or more of snow did she utter a sharp yell, and even then it had more of rage in it than complaint.

Susan leaped after her; the two men below caught her between them, and the shock of the cold gripped her to the waist and made her gasp.

'Get away from the hulk,' cried McHugh, motioning peremptorily; and confused with snow and darkness, in a formless world which as yet they could not even see, Miranda and Susan took arms and struggled laboriously through the drifts to a safe distance. The first of the men was being lifted bodily out of the doorway and held clear of the aircraft's side. They recognised the shape of Richard Hellier.

'Easy with him, the old chap's had a knock on the head. Case fell on him – a bit dazed, but all right. Ready?''

He was hardly heavier than Susan; they received him into their arms gently, and Susan waded back to meet him and draw him aside. He let her take his arm, and followed where she led with the silent docility of shock or concussion. Looking back, she saw that they were all out now. McHugh came last, his coat flying about him. They gathered shivering in a close little knot, well apart from the plane, and drew breath at last.

'Close thing,' said McHugh, and swiped a coat sleeve across his forhead. 'Everybody all right?'

There was no time yet for recognising the existence

of cold or discomfort; to be alive was to be all right. They said that they were, with no dissentient voice, until Richard, suddenly stirring out of his daze, shivered and clapped a hand under his arm. 'My briefcase! Where did I leave my briefcase?' His voice, that beautiful, resonant voice which for ten years now, since it had lost its full range and tone, had resolutely refused to sing, even in private, held a childish distress and dismay. 'I'm sorry, but I must go back. I left my briefcase behind.'

McHugh put a restraining hand on his arm. 'You can't go back in there now. Nobody's going to disturb your things, but we can't risk fetching them yet. Got to find somewhere to spend the night, and get you under cover. We'll collect everything later, don't worry.'

'No, I can't leave it. You don't understand, I can't go without my briefcase—'

'If it had been going to take fire it would have done it by now,' said Neil abruptly. 'I'll go and fetch his briefcase, why not? It won't take a minute.'

McHugh considered, looking back at the grotesque hulk lying in the snow, its shape already obscured by the steady, smothering fall. 'Well, I don't think anything will happen now. We're through the worst. All right, if you want to, I'll come and give you a shoulder to get up.'

'I'm exceedingly sorry,' said Richard contritely, in that dazed, punctilious voice of shock. 'So stupid of me to leave it behind. Please don't take any risk—'

McHugh patted his arm reassuringly. 'I don't think there's much risk now. The landing was touch and go, but we've got off lightly. You hang on here a minute.'

Neil had struck out ahead of him into the snow-field, trekking back by the wavering pathway they had cut through the drifts, wallowing and falling and rising again. The aeroplane lay half-veiled in the slanting fall. It seemed to have settled lower already, for the silting flakes were climbing its flanks steadily, and settling in a smooth wave within the open doorway. Neil was the lighter weight of the two. McHugh gave him a back to reach the step, and waited, shivering now in reaction, as he vanished into the darkness within. He was invisible for some minutes. After a while, tired of inaction, McHugh measured the distance to the doorway. It was not so difficult; on his best form he could get up there without troubling anyone for a hoist. He made a leap for it, got a firm grip of the edge, and hauled himself steadily up until he could get a knee over the sill.

'What's the matter? Can't you find it?'

The pencil-thin shaft of light from Neil's pocket torch played over a huddle of fallen raincoats, and the corner of the open briefcase. He was just thrusting back the splayed contents and snapping the catch upon them.

'Yes, I've got it. Burst the thing open when it was pitched off the rack. I hope everything's there, or the old boy will probably refuse to budge. Get below and I'll drop it to you. I'm going to bring my own, too, now I'm here.'

'Oh, yes, the old girl's will,' said McHugh cheerfully, dropping back easily into the snow. 'Can't leave that around unguarded, with all these potential heirs about. All right, throw it!'

He picked the two cases out of the air casually as they came down, and stowed them under his arm.

A moment later Neil was beside him.

'Where are we going to make for now? We've got to get these people under cover somewhere for the night. You don't happen to know roughly where we are?'

'Not even roughly. But I do know there were lights below there, so there must be a village. It looked quite close, but the way down may take some finding. Let's hope they've heard us come down. If they have, they'll be out looking for us. Come on, we'd better get 'em moving.'

The bowl of meadows, high towards the passes over the ridges, showed now as a faint shape in the murk. Smooth under the heavy snows, the great white slopes curved upwards all around them. It was not difficult to find the one downward incline; and if there was indeed a village, somewhere down there it must lie. In just such a lofty bowl as this the cattle and pigs from a village might be pastured through the summer; but if there were huts here they were entirely under the snow now. However, shapes and planes took on significance as their eyes grew used to the faint, veiled darkness. All the lines of the inclined bowl drew down into one descending point, as the veins of a leaf into its stem.

'This way,' said McHugh, clambering and thrusting clumsily down into the gully and marshalling his flock after him. They followed mutely, shivering with cold and shock, but clinging tenaciously at his heels. They would not always be so united.

The way down to the village, obscured by drifts and invisible and treacherous everywhere, might have taken them three or four hours unaided, though in summer it must have been about half an hour's brisk walking. But they were fortunate. After half an hour of painful and cautious progress, exhausted, wet, chilled to the bone, they halted for the third breather, and McHugh cupped his hands about his mouth and hallooed down towards the dark valley; and faintly and clearly from the distance came an answering shout. A quarter of an hour later they saw the moving lights winding upwards to meet them.

Large, steady figures, thick as boulders, loomed out of the night. In the light of the first lantern they saw a bearded face, a great white-toothed grin. Miranda heaved a sob of weariness, and illogically began to cry. Laurence put his arm round her shoulders, and said soothingly: 'It's all right, Mother, everything's all right now.'

'*Grüss Gott!*' said the smiling mouth gently, in a voice that seemed to come out of the roots of the mountains, and quick eyes looked them over, counting. '*Alles?*'

'*Alles,*' said McHugh, wiping his streaming face. '*Gott sei dank!*'

'*Gott sei dank! Kommen Sie mit,*' said the voice, '*da unten ist unser Dorf, da können Sie ruhen.*'

CHAPTER III

The statutes are precise. No way is known of circumventing them.

Act 1

Oberschwandegg was a couple of dozen beetle-browed houses clustered about a tiny triangular open space and a short street, as many enclosed yards full of stock and fodder and firewood, a minute church with an onion dome on top of a little tower, and outer walls with a batter strong as a fortress, and one sprawling inn, the Horse in the Meadows. It sat securely in the one level space in the valley, which for the remainder of its length rushed precipitately downhill towards Bad Schwandegg thirteen kilometres below.

The track that joined them was hardly ever passable except on foot or by mule, being narrow, jagged, and forked like a lightning flash among its rocks. In winter it could not be tackled on skis without considerable risk even in good, sound snow, and under a big fall it was sealed altogether, sometimes for two or three weeks at a time. They were used to it; they made provision accordingly every autumn. At a pinch they could do very well without posts, police, and all the other amenities of modern life which were cut off with the outer world.

In any case they made little enough use of them even when they were available. Most of what they wanted they found at home, even wives.

The village sat rooted firmly on its mountain shelf, waist-deep in snow, drifts leaning here and there against the shutters of upper windows. It had snowed heavily and ceaselessly ever since it began at about three o'clock of the previous afternoon, on a veering wind that had taken everybody by surprise; and at six o'clock this evening it was snowing still. The one telephone line was down, somewhere below there, out of reach. The track was already snowed under, metres deep. Oberschwandegg was an island in the sky. Later, if the temperature dropped considerably and brought sharp enough frost, the fall might stop for some hours; but the sky was full of it, and before morning it would be falling again.

Franz Mehlert eyed the sagging clouds, counted over his swollen household, newly increased by eight unexpected guests, and reckoned his stores adequate for a month. It was unlikely that they would be cut off as long as that.

All the same, it was going to be a difficult Christmas. Eight out-of-season guests were a profitable present from heaven, though he would not have chosen to acquire them in quite this way; but these eight, fresh from a funeral and all too plainly with nothing in common among them but their expectations from the dead, had brought no blessings into the house in their salvaged baggage. Not even the simple blessing of gratitude for their lives. Or if they had, they had mislaid it overnight.

Susan, in flight from Miranda's querulous company, would have agreed with him heartily. She tried the door of the small private dining room, only to come upon Trevor Mason and Dr Randall still feverishly outbidding each other over a chessboard and tea laced with rum. Trevor's long, nervous fingers were clenched in his thick iron-grey hair,and his hollow, mobile, comedian's face was sad.

'Without saying she was anything but shrewd herself,' he was saying, 'I can really claim that she owed her fortune to me. I know how considerable it is. I should, I built it for her. I remember she once said to me—'

Susan closed the door again hurriedly. She had no wish to be drawn into that contest either as referee or audience. They were like jealous children, each of them waiting confidently for a compliment from the dead which would floor his opponent for the count, and each of them ready to take it hideously to heart and grieve over it for life if he did not get it. It wasn't only in her youth, it wasn't only in her lifetime, that Antonia had known how to drive men crazy.

In the little glassed-in terrace room over the street someone was playing the piano very softly to himself, and singing in a slightly husky, hesitant voice. She recognised one of the Loewe songs Antonia had frequently included in her recitals. 'Süsses Begräbnis' ('Sweet Repose'). Did Antonia enjoy sweet repose now? After a lifetime of mischief it seemed a dull prospect for her. Surely there was a cat left somewhere for her to toss in among the pigeons.

Laurence looked up quickly as the door opened, scowling suspiciously over the piano, but his face cleared a little when he recognised Susan. He even

29

smiled, though in a preoccupied way. He was not really a bad-looking young man when he smiled.

'Oh, hullo!' He finished the accompaniment meticulously, looking down at his rippling fingers from under lowered lashes. 'You've heard there's a real Christmas dinner laid on for us tonight? Liesl's just putting the finishing touches to the tree. What a pity we've got nothing to put under it. What would you like for Christmas?'

Susan closed the door behind her and crossed the room to lean on the upright piano. The eerie reflected light from the snow poured in through the glass wall and glowed along the pale panelling. I know, she thought, what the rest of you would like, but thank God that doesn't involve me.

'You know what I'd like?' he pursued clairvoyantly, his hands still busy. 'You'd never guess! A beautiful *cor anglais*! It was always the horn I really wanted to play. I hated the piano right from my first lesson, and I always shall.'

'I can hardly believe that,' said Susan, surprised, 'or you wouldn't play it so well.'

'Oh, why not? You don't have to love things to be good at them. You can master anything if you really have to.'

'And you had to?' She could imagine it, though it had never occurred to her to wonder about him until now. She saw a sullen but subdued little boy sitting reluctantly at the piano hour after hour, with his mother persistent and dogged at his elbow, nagging at him if he tried to sneak away a minute too soon, and probably rapping his knuckles with her steel knitting needles if he played a wrong note.

'What do you think?' He looked up suddenly into

her face, an indignant flush on his cheekbones, as though he could read her thoughts, and see only too clearly the picture she was seeing. 'My mother couldn't see any future in the horn. You can't use the horn to accompany rich old sopranos who may, if you're good, leave you a lot of money.'

There was a moment of astonished silence, while he glared challengingly at her, and she looked back at him without a word to say. Then he shrugged, and gave her a grudging smile. 'Oh, it's all right, I can't blame you for feeling that way. I couldn't very well help knowing it, you know. And anyhow, it's true. I was groomed for that job for years.'

'I'm afraid,' said Susan with surprised sympathy, 'you haven't enjoyed it.'

'You mustn't blame my mother too much,' he said rather stiffly. 'She's always been poor, and since I was nine she's had to fend for herself and me. It took a lot of scraping and saving to educate me, though you may not think much of the end product. It warps your thinking if you're not careful. Even when my father was alive he wasn't a good provider, and he didn't treat her too well. I was always determined not to take over where he left off. So I couldn't kick, she had the drop on me every time.' He flexed his fingers ruefully, and began to play the introduction to 'Frühlingsglaube'. 'Even now I can't afford to stop practising. I'm out of a job.'

It seemed silly to avoid mentioning Antonia's money any longer; it was a reality, and so was his honest claim on it. 'You surely won't have to worry too much about a job,' said Susan directly, 'once the will's settled.'

There was no doubt about it, this boy was

31

hypersensitive on the subject of his prospects from that quarter. He gave her one quick, dark look, and frowned down at his fingers again more blackly than ever. 'I don't want her money. No, that's a lie, too. I should like to be well off, who wouldn't? But I'd rather she left it to a cats' home than have it willed to me as pay for putting up with her humbly for three years. I don't want to be paid! She paid me quite generously while she was alive. I earned that, and I got it.'

'Look!' said Susan, her chin on her fists, 'why did you stay with her?'

He snatched back his hands furiously, and glared up at her with hazel eyes fierce and yellow as a cat's. 'I know damn' well why you think I stayed with her!'

'You don't know anything of the kind! I don't know myself, that's why I'm asking you. But you're not going to tell me it was for love.'

'No, it wasn't! I didn't love her. But I *did like* her, believe it or not. And I respected her, too. She was an old demon, but hell, she could sing! She could sing most lieder singers off the stage, even at seventy-six, and that was only the wreckage of what she had been. I wouldn't leave a woman who could sing like that, not until she threw me out. She made accompanying worth my while.' He slammed down the lid of the piano with a challenging crash. 'But you won't believe that!'

'Yes, I will,' snapped back Susan, herself astonished to find it true, 'I do. I've always known you were a real musician, she wouldn't have kept you on if you hadn't been. But I'd believe you just as willingly if you'd just tell me things, instead of hurling them at me like grenades.'

32

He stared at her for a moment with a confused face, half ashamed and half resentful, and then he bounded to his feet, grinning, and reached a hand for hers across the piano. 'Come and have a drink! Quick, before my mother comes and winkles me out of here to smarten myself up for dinner. She won't look in the bar, she'd feel it wasn't quite nice for her to be seen in there.'

He was too late. Miranda's high-pitched voice, at once imperious and querulous, was calling his name from the foot of the stairs. 'Oh, *God!*' said Laurence, clutching a handful of his straw-coloured hair. 'I knew I'd never get by in a sweater. She's a great one for keeping up standards. Now what'll I do?'

'Better go. We'll have the drink after dinner.'

'That's a date?'

'That's a date. Maybe we could sneak out for a breath of air if it stops snowing. I could do with one.'

'I know just how you feel,' said Laurence heartily, and grinned at her and fled, closing the door gently to preserve her solitude for her; apparently he really did know just how she felt. Why on earth, she thought, doesn't he smile more often? He could be quite attractive.

She waited until the hall was quiet, and then went up to her front room on the wooden verandah to put on a pretty dress for the party. After all, it was Christmas Eve. The wreath with its red ribbons and coloured candles hung in the hall, from Frau Mehlert's kitchen a warm scent of vanilla sugar and baking pervaded the whole house, and Liesl had put in a great deal of thought on dressing the table for them and decorating a second little tree. And they had already received their Christmas presents; they

were alive, that was cause enough for celebration,
surely.

Nevertheless, the party was not a success. Miranda
came down in a fashionable black dress, and its
shapelessness hung upon her shapelessness
dejectedly. She wore her usual three-row necklet of
seed pearls, and her mouse-grey hair was as rigidly
waved as ever. Laurence had allowed himself to be
bullied into a dark suit, and the scowl was back on
his brow, though now it looked more like apprehension than ill temper, and perhaps the look of roused
determination on his mother's face had a great deal
to do with it. Thwarted in her evident design to
secure the seat next to Neil Everard, she placed
herself firmly opposite to him across the table, and
Laurence seated himself dutifully beside her. Or was
it rather that he wanted to be where he could
whisper in her ear or lay a hand on her arm at need?
She looked as though she might need to be restrained
before the meal was over.

But it was the memory of Antonia that presided
over the table like an incalculable ghost. Her hand
was on every one of them. Richard sat silent, buried
in his own thoughts. After years of love and understanding he needed no demonstration of her favour,
nor could anything she might have left him replace
what he had lost. But the rest! Susan could feel the
threads of tension and speculation tightening
between them before the carp was on the table. No
wonder Laurence was making free with the wine.

'She was a wonderful woman,' said Miranda
firmly, taking the conversation out of Trevor's hands
before he had time to conclude his latest recollection
of the deceased. 'No one knows it better than I, I

lived on the closest terms with her. She had great qualities. But one should not let the truth be obscured – I'm sure Aunt Antonia herself would be the first to confess that she was not perfect. One had to admit that she could be capricious at times, even inconsiderate. She had been used to taking everything as her right, of course, she couldn't realise how much she exacted from other people in effort and devotion.' She drank deliberately, her eyes upon Neil. 'Could one rely on gratitude from such a person? I can't help wondering.'

Laurence muttered: 'Mother, not tonight!'

'Yes, dear, tonight. After all, this is a simple matter of business. It can't matter to Mr Everard whether it's discharged here or in London. And he'll surely understand that it's of great importance to us. We've lost our home and our livelihood, we shall have problems and expenses waiting for us when we get to England, and we're not wealthy, why pretend we are? I gave years of my life to her, I have a right to expect some consideration in return. And so has my son, Mr Everard, after all his services to her, though I think she never fully appreciated how great his contribution was.'

'Mother, please! Damn it, I was paid well enough—' He was writhing and glowering, but maybe he was speculating, too. At any rate, he let himself be ridden over.

'Be quiet, Laurence, and let me speak. I'm not asking any special favours, Mr Everard, only that this uncertainty shall be ended. We are Aunt Antonia's only relatives and her closest friends—'

'Some of us might question if the two are necessarily the same thing,' said Trevor Mason tartly.

'As a matter of fact, I was speaking of all of us here, Mr Mason. Or at least, of Mr Hellier and Dr Randall. Your relationship with her was of course a business one—'

'And yours was not?' he said drily.

'I say that all the people who were closest to Aunt Antonia are here now, and since there's no help for this delay, and we don't know how long it may go on, I think we all have a right to know exactly where we stand. Mr Everard, I appeal to you, should not the will be read now, tonight? We have to make plans for the future, and how can we when we have no idea what our resources are to be?'

'It's a matter for you people,' said Neil austerely. 'Since we were all going home there seemed no point in dealing with it until my uncle could handle it himself in London. But certainly the situation's changed now. We don't know how long we're going to be here, and it might very well be better to clear up any doubts. What do the rest of you think?'

Dr Randall lifted his shoulders. 'It's a matter of indifference to me, now or later, as you like.'

Richard came out of his dream long enough to look round at them all vaguely, as though they were the unreality. 'Do as you think best, my dear boy, I don't mind.'

'The sooner the better,' said Trevor succinctly. 'Susan?'

'Doesn't concern me,' said Susan cheerfully, helping herself from Liesl's dish of almond cakes.

'Oh, yes, it does. You're mentioned in the will, too.'

Miranda bristled, adding one more to the tale of legacies to be deducted from her fortune. Susan swallowed a gulp of suprise, and then shrugged off the astonishment philosophically. A small conventional acknowledgement to an employee, that was all it could be.

'I'll go along with the rest, then. Why not tonight, and get it over?'

'Very well,' said Neil. 'As soon as we've finished dinner I'll fetch it. I'll have a word with Herr Mehlert, and make sure we can have this room to ourselves.' He had not, Susan noticed, asked Laurence his views; presumably Miranda was considered to have spoken for both of them.

Neil went up to his room, and brought down the long envelope that contained Antonia's new will. McHugh, grinning, finished his coffee and pushed back his chair. 'Well, this lets me out. If any of you lucky people likes to buy me a double brandy later, I'll be in the bar.'

He closed the door with a brisk slam, and they were left tensed over their coffee cups, watching one another covertly across the table, and quivering to the rustling of the thick paper as Neil unfolded the will. In the long, close passages they caught glimpses of Antonia's fine, affected hand, perfected as a part of her public character, and a source of amusement to her in her private one. 'It will look magnificent in the biographies,' she used to say complacently, dashing off the same accomplished signature at the end of a letter. The witnesses to it in this case had been the manager of the hotel and the chambermaid. I suppose I might have known, thought Susan, by her not asking me, that I was going to be a beneficiary. She felt herself quivering with the others, and was alarmed. How easy it was to fall into the habit of coveting money, once it was dangled within reach.

'There are several minor bequests to old servants and so on,' said Neil, 'but I'd better read the whole of it.'

He began in a dry voice, purposely detaching himself from them. A hundred pounds to the old woman who had been her dresser for years, the same to the housekeeper of her house in Kent, a great number of personal souvenirs to scattered friends. He came at last to the meat, and the tone of his voice stiffened perceptibly, their nerves stretching with it.

' "—to my secretary, Susan Conroy, the sum of one hundred pounds—" '

Susan breathed again, blessedly neither elated or disappointed. A new outfit for job-hunting, she thought contentedly, and leisure to look round; that was nice of the old girl, and more than I could have expected even if I'd expected anything. And so readily does the mind adjust itself to self-interest that she almost ceased to listen until she heard the names of Trevor Mason and Dr Randall coupled closely together. ' "My friend and manager—" ' ' "—Dr Charles Randall, to whom I am indebted for many years of devoted care—" ' She had left them five hundred pounds each, without a word of warmth or the gift of one personal possession. Trevor's comedian's mask had grown long and pale with offence. He had not expected to get her collection of letters and manuscript music, not while Richard was alive, but he had hoped for the Sargent portrait of her as a girl; she had known, none better, how much he loved it.

' "—to my niece, Miranda Ruth Quayne, the sum of one thousand pounds—" ' ' "—to her son, my

great-nephew Laurence Quayne, the sum of one
thousand pounds—" '

It sounds quite a lot of money, provided you have
not been looking forward confidently to a quarter
of a million, and security for life. Miranda drew a
gasping breath, and Laurence caught her by the arm
under the tablecloth, and dug his fingers into her
flesh so hard that she winced. His eyelids were
lowered over the hazel eyes, and his face was alert
and still; it was impossible to guess what he was
feeling, apart from the ferocity with which he was
willing his mother to keep her mouth shut.

' "—all the residue of my real and personal estate
whatsoever and wheresoever I give, devise, and
bequeath to my dear friend Richard Hellier
absolutely; and should the said Richard Hellier
predecease me or die intestate, the said residue shall
be divided equally between the following five
legatees: Susan Conroy, Trevor Amphlett Mason,
Charles Randall, Miranda Ruth Quayne, and
Laurence Quayne." '

That, in effect, was all, and more than enough.
Only the cold paralysis of shock kept Miranda quiet
while Neil's carefully restrained voice read to the
end. There was a stupefied silence, which Richard
was the first to break. His thin, lined face was drawn
into a mask of bewilderment and consternation.

'But why? What possessed her?' he said helplessly.
'She knew I had enough. She knew—' He stopped
there, suddenly clenching his hands on the arms of
his chair and thrusting himself to his feet. He looked
round at them all, and saw envy and resentment
staring back at him, and for a moment the sum of
those looks felt very like naked hate. 'I think I'd

39

better withdraw to the bar, too,' he said bitterly, 'so that you can talk about me in comfort.'

He was already at the door when Laurence found his voice.

'Richard, don't go! I should like—'

But Richard was gone, and the door had closed decidedly after him.

CHAPTER IV

But why think of death?
'Tis far from hence!

Act 2

They were all talking at once, but Miranda was the loudest, shrillest, and angriest, and her lament rode high above the more temperate complaints of Trevor and the doctor. She was on her feet, trembling with rage, and shaking off Laurence's restraining hand violently.

'Mr Everard, this is monstrous! She must have been out of her mind to make such a will, and it's my belief it could be upset by the courts, and ought to be, in mere justice. It isn't *right*! Is this my reward for years of devoted service? It was always understood that she would at least make reasonable provision for her own. What right has that old man to filch a fortune from under the noses of her relatives?'

'Mother, do be reasonable, Richard hasn't filched anything, he's as staggered about it as you are, you heard him. Even if she did turn her back on you, it isn't his fault. He's just as upset as anyone else—'

She turned on him like a fury. 'Upset? It's all very well to profess to be upset when you're a quarter of a million better off. It costs nothing at all to sound righteous about it. Don't tell me he knew nothing

41

about it. And don't touch me! I won't be hushed! Her own niece, to be rebuffed at the end like this! Her own flesh and blood, her only female relative! In very decency her jewellery should have come to me. Mr Everard, I insist that you take this up with your uncle. You must see that it can't be left like this. She was not in full possession of her faculties—'

'I'm afraid,' said Neil stiffly, folding the will back into its envelope, 'that you'll have very considerable difficulty in upholding that argument. I saw a great deal of Mrs Byrne during the last days of her illness, and I had Dr Randall's advice throughout. She was perfectly clear and entirely capable when she dictated the terms of that will, and I assure you it will stand up in any court. I sympathise with your disappointment, but there's nothing I can do about it. It's not for me to try to influence my clients, only to ensure that their wishes are clearly expressed and properly carried out.'

'I'm afraid, Mrs Quayne,' said Dr Randall flatly, 'that you are contending only with a capricious old woman, not a feeble-minded one. There's no legal protection against ingratitude.'

'But her jewellery!' Tears of frustration and yearning were running down Miranda's powdered cheeks, the elaborately waved head trembled uncontrollably. 'That at least should have stayed in the family, it isn't decent to will it away like that. The archduke's diamonds not even mentioned! The only honourable thing the wicked old woman could have done with them was to hand them on to her own relations, and she doesn't even say one word about them. I demand that you take some steps to contest this iniquitous will, or at the very least to point out to Mr Hellier the *impropriety* of accepting the archduke's diamonds. He has an absolute *obligation* to release them to me, he'll surely see that.'

'Mother,' said Laurence desperately, 'for God's sake leave the damn' will alone, we don't need her money—'

'Don't be a fool!' she snapped at him furiously. 'It isn't just the money, it's the principle of the thing. Those diamonds—'

'My dear Mrs Quayne,' said Neil, controlling his detestation as well as he could, 'you're living in a fool's paradise if you're relying on those legends about diamonds.'

'Nonsense, everyone knows she had them. They must be in the safekeeping of your firm, it's useless to deny it.'

'I see it is, but nonetheless I do deny it. I have never seen them, Mrs Byrne never discussed them or even mentioned them in my presence. My father discounted the stories, and very certainly never had any such stones through his hands. He did not believe in their existence, and neither do I. Is that plain enough for you, Mrs Quayne?'

It was more than she could bear. All her life she had been waiting hopefully in the conviction that the diamonds existed, and that some day they would come to her. If they were no more than a flourish in a garbled story, then the very earth was crumbling under her feet. Rather than believe that she would clutch at any alternative, however monstrous. She took a frantic step forward, flourishing her bony fists in Neil's face.

'They *did* exist! If they're nowhere to be found

now, it's because you've made away with them – misappropriated them to your own use—'

'Mother!' bellowed Laurence, suddenly releasing all his hoarded anguish in one outburst of rage. '*Shut up!*'

She turned on him a face of ludicrous astonishment, and drew breath to annihilate him, but he caught her by the shoulders and shook her before she could get out a word. 'Shut up, I said. You're making an unpleasant fool of yourself. If you feel like apologising to Neil for what you just said, all right – otherwise be quiet. The whole thing's over and done with – you understand? She could leave her own property to anyone she fancied, and she has done, and that's that.' He bit off the consonant viciously, and looked at Neil over her quivering shoulder. 'I'm sorry, Neil! I apologise for my mother, she's hysterical.'

'Don't give it a thought,' said Neil quietly. 'I promise I shan't.' He turned and stalked out of the room, his back rigid with forbearance, and in a moment they heard him climbing the stairs.

Miranda began to cry noisily, the hard, disfiguring tears of rage. She pushed Laurence away from her, hitting at him weakly. 'Much support I ever get from you! You're just like your father! Why did I ever bother about you?'

'Mother, please control yourself. It's no use going on like this. Hadn't you better go to bed?'

'I will not go to bed,' she shrilled. 'You heartless, ungrateful boy, where would you have been without me? Haven't I the right to expect some loyalty from you, after all I've done for you? And now you've turned out good for nothing, just like your father!'

He took his hands from her and stood back, pale as wax, breathing hard. 'Maybe the best thing I can do is take to drink, like my father, too,' he said in a very quiet voice. 'At least you'd get a kind of satisfaction out of that.' And he swung on his heel and marched out of the room without another glance at her, and made for the bar as though his life depended on it.

It was wonderfully noisy and wonderfully good-humoured in the warm, panelled room among the villagers of Oberschwandegg. Great earthy voices conversed at full pitch in a dialect he could not follow, but he felt their exchanges to be closer and more welcome to his heart than any English he had heard since Antonia had died. Except, perhaps, Susan's blunt voice saying that she believed him, and that he needn't shout about it. He leaned an elbow on the bar, and ordered a large schnapps, and the very voice he had just been remembering said gently over his shoulder: 'Make it two!'

He looked round at her apologetically.

'We had a date, remember?'

'So we did,' he said, and managed a slightly mangled smile. When he passed her glass back to her he was astonished to find that his hand was shaking absurdly; and even after she had installed them both in a corner by the great stove of unglazed white ceramic, with its indented radiation eyes glazed in amber, he sat trembling with nervous tension for some minutes before he could talk to her.

'I saw my father hit her,' he said at last in a low voice, twisting the glass round and round on the scrubbed table. 'Three times in his life. I used to think he was a brute. Now I wonder!'

'Cheer up!' said Susan simply. 'You didn't hit her. It's all over now.'

'Bar the shouting,' said Laurence bitterly. 'That I shall be hearing for some time. Bloody lucky if I ever hear the last of it.'

She did not care to say what was obvious, that he ought to get away from her. Clearly he knew it without being told. Maybe he would have done it, if Antonia had seen fit to leave her a competence, but now even that was out of the question. Somebody had to keep Miranda, she would never be able to earn her own living, and what was a mere thousand pounds? Susan could think of nothing more practical to do in this situation than carry his empty glass back to the bar and bring him a second schnapps. What did it matter if he got a little tight? Things might look better to him that way. He downed the second as promptly as the first, and recovered a little of his colour.

'Christmas Eve!' he said. 'Poor old Trevor didn't get much of a Christmas box, either, did he? And I happen to know he could use a little margin at the moment, too. He hasn't always been as careful for himself in the markets as he was for Aunt Antonia. Funny it should work that way.'

Susan looked through the crevice of the shutters and saw the swathes of snow pale in their own lambent light along the village street, and a knot of stars through torn cloud. 'It's stopped snowing. Would you like that breath of air?'

'*Would* I!'

'Run and get your coat, then. I've got mine down in the hall already.'

He went with alacrity, like a boy let out of school.

46

When he came down she was waiting for him at the foot of the stairs, straight and dark in the candlelight from the hanging wreath, her hands deep in the pockets of a boyish duffle coat, and the collar turned up to her ears. Their footsteps rang together hastily on the bare boards of the floor, and because they went with their chins on their shoulders, apprehensive of being called back into the dining room if they did not make good their escape quickly, they walked full tilt into McHugh, who was just emerging from the open doorway of the little terrace room opposite the bar.

He had a liqueur glass in his hand, and a puzzled grin on his face, and he, too, was looking back over his shoulder. At one of the small tables by the glass wall Richard sat writing, a large beer mug before him, and the fellow of McHugh's brandy glass at his elbow, also plainly waiting for his attention. The snow looked in at him, glittering with cold, though the little room was warm and snug.

'Fairly knocks you!' confided McHugh, recovering his balance and deftly swinging his glass out of danger. 'What d'you think the old boy's just told me? Comes into the bar upset as the devil, and downs one litre like a professional and asks for another and some writing paper, and off he goes in there by himself. I just took him the fellow to this tot here, and he gets talkative. He's properly upset about this legacy. Says what on earth did she do a thing like that for, without saying a word to him. Says she knew very well he had enough of his own, and didn't want any more.'

'I know,' said Laurence shortly. 'I hope to God he isn't going to start fretting about it.'

'I never thought of a quarter of a million as something you'd have to get over,' said McHugh. 'And know what that is he's writing? His will! He's making a will! He's just asked me if I'll be one of his witnesses when he's finished it. Says he'll make damned sure nobody cherishes any hopes of his dying intestate!' He shook his head helplessly over the incomprehensible actions and reactions of his troublesome cargo, and drifted away into the bar, still grinning.

Laurence moved on towards the outer door, but in an instant checked again and looked back at the solitary old man bent over his pen. The silver fringe of hair round his bald crown caught the glitter of frost from outside the window. The long profile, still clear and handsome, stood sharply outlined against the half-opaque whiteness of the glass, and on the steadily writing hand the small pink glow of the table lamp hung motionless, a spotlight drawing down the whole drama of Antonia's death and its repercussions into one small sheet of paper.

'Will you wait for me a moment?' said Laurence abruptly, and was off into the room before she could answer, threading his way resolutely between the tables. She stood in the doorway and watched him as he came to Richard's elbow. His voice echoed back to her clearly, a little constrained but very determined.

'Mr Hellier, I just wanted to congratulate you, and to tell you I'm glad. I'm glad my aunt knew an honest man from a shark when she saw one. I'm glad she didn't feel obliged to leave her money in the family if she didn't want to. She didn't owe me anything, and I didn't count on anything from her. I just wanted you to know, and – not to feel bad about it.'

Richard had looked up to arm himself, and now was unexpectedly disarmed. 'My dear boy!' he said somewhat blankly. 'My dear boy!' But Laurence had already turned and was heading back to the doorway with a heightened colour and an elastic step, as if he had cast some part at least of the weight of his depression.

'Come on!' he said with considerably more self-confidence than he would have shown five minutes earlier, and took her arm very firmly and marched her out into the sparkling night. They fell into step together instinctively, and drew great breaths of the cold, clear air. Around them there was an enormous, grateful calm. The temperature was only a degree or two below freezing, and with first light there would surely be heavy cloud and renewed snow; but now it was lucid and still, and full of soft, dilated stars.

The snow was a metre deep and more on the open green, where it was undisturbed, and narrow paths, cut down cleanly through the fall, linked every house to the broader track which was all that remained of the village street. Under the low, jutting eaves the half-shuttered windows shed bars of tinted light like golden ladders along the snow, and evergreen wreaths hung on the doors. Somewhere a very small band, perhaps five or six musicians, was playing 'Maria auf dem Berge' and shrill little voices were singing:

'Auf dem Berge da wehet der Wind,
Da wiegt Maria ihr Kind.
Sie wiegt ihn mit ihrer schneeweisen Hand
Sie hat dazu kein Wiegenband—'

Susan took up the Virgin's part, very softly, as they walked, and back came Laurence's hesitant baritone, gruff with shyness, answering for Joseph.

'Feel better now?'

'Much better!' But he was going to hate going back to the Horse in the Meadows.

They walked to the far end of the village, past the last lighted window, and came to where the track ended in a great waste of snow. The level of the ground declined, but tortuously, among faces of rock now buried and smoothed in snow, great twisted planes of lambent whiteness. Far away below, where all shapes were lost in darkness, they caught glimpses of the lights of the lower world, where Bad Schwandegg, hardly bigger than its lofty twin, squatted in its sheltered valley. They could see, but could not communicate. Between their eyrie and the world flowed the great snow ocean. They drew close together and were very still, staring across the impassable barrier.

'You're not cold?' asked Laurence.

'No, thanks, I'm fine. Let's go and look in the church, shall we?'

All the trodden paths from all the village converged upon the church; at midnight everyone would be there, except the littlest children and the grandparents who must stay at home to mind them. They approached the open gate arm in arm, slipping and recovering in the rutted track. The building stood on an unbelievably small plot of ground, and reared up tall as the trees, almost more steeple than church. The high white walls splayed outward at the foot into thick, short buttresses, and the two tiers of windows were small and square, sunk deep into the masonry like shot windows in a fortress. The roof was very high and steep, and had already shed the day's snow in two lateral waves. Only a thin silver glitter of frost filmed over its crimson tiles. Within, the walls were as white as without, and almost as bare of native ornament, but they were hung now with evergreens and stuck with candles, and the warmth and fragrance of the fir branches and the cones made the air heady and drunken. So short was the nave that when they entered the doorway it seemed they could stretch out their hands and touch the crucifix on the spiky little baroque altar. Someone in this very village must have carved that wooden Christ, maybe nearly three centuries ago; it had the air of a native, the rooted look, the clarity and the sturdiness. It was also beautiful, with the directness of the unself-conscious. The market for tourist carvings even now did not reach as far as Oberschwandegg. They carved for themselves here, and never stopped to wonder if their methods would tickle anyone else's fancy.

The crib near the door was old, too, perhaps older than the altar, a little wooden stage set of a stable, a manger cradle, and small painted figures of men and angels and animals, worn glossy with long years of handling, and thickened by many renewed coats of paint. They were peasant figures, the Virgin as stout and bucolic as the shepherds, the Child miraculously free from the amorphous prettiness of later confections. A little girl, swathed to the eyes in a big shawl, had lifted the ox and the lamb out of the crib, and was nursing and petting them in her arms.

It was warm in the church. Susan and Laurence

sat down in a retired corner at the back, and stayed there for a long time in silence, curiously content. When at last they rose and took the road back to the inn it was nearly midnight, and the stir of excitement was quivering through the village like a fresh wind. They met whole families marching through the snow with lanterns, and returned their greetings gladly. The little band, still invisible in some enclosed yard, was playing 'Es ist ein Ros' entsprungen'.

'Listen!' said Susan, shutting her fingers on his arm. 'A horn!'

He halted with her, smiling, to follow the solemn, lovely tune to its noble close. The horn made a beautiful, round, resonant sound in the frosty stillness.

'The last one. They'll stop now, and go to church.' And as he had foretold, silence came after, and along the track they saw the muffled figures with their instruments hurrying out of a low wooden gateway and making for the church. 'Oh, God, I wish we needn't go in,' said Laurence abruptly. 'But I suppose somebody'd miss us and start a panic. And you must be tired.'

'They'll all have gone to bed,' said Susan comfortingly. 'And tomorrow's Christmas Day. Peace on earth to men of goodwill!'

'Between the lot of us we seem to be horribly short on goodwill,' said Laurence bitterly, 'so maybe we can't expect much peace.'

At the yard gate they met Herr and Frau Mehlert and Liesl in their festival clothes, and wished them a Merry Christmas. The side door of the house, it seemed, was fastened, but the front door was still open for them. They rounded the corner with slowing steps, reluctant to go in, and the flood of light from the terrace room fell obliquely across their path and made them look up sharply.

'There's one who hasn't gone to bed,' said Laurence, 'though it looks as if he's fallen asleep.'

Richard was still sitting at his table, his forearms spread on either side of the empty cognac glass, his chin sunk on his breast. Old men easily nod off in comfortable chairs, and the little room was overheated, if anything, in spite of having the appearance of an aquarium tank.

'Cognac on top of two litres of pretty good beer,' said Laurence, shaking his head. 'Maybe I'd better see him up to bed.'

'If the family had come out by this way they'd have noticed him and wakened him,' said Susan, kicking off clods of snow before mounting the steps. 'If the door of that room's closed they'd never see from the hall that the light was still on. This is a land where doors really fit.'

She stepped into darkness and warmth and the heavy scent of fir branches and wax candles, and halted for a moment, groping for the light switch. Laurence closed the outer door behind them, and felt for it, too, over her shoulder. Her warmth touched his breast. He felt her breath on his cheek.

It was not designed, it happened as naturally as the contact of their bodies in the dark. His arm went round her gently, his lips touched her cheek and fumbled their way inexpertly but delicately to her mouth. She neither withdrew from his kiss nor returned it; and though her groping fingers had found the switch, she did not put on the light. For a long moment they hung still, then he drew back rather clumsily, as though a sudden recoil into timidity had made him repent his act.

When she snapped on the light her face was just as he had feared it would be, placid and undisturbed, the straight stare of her dark eyes disconcerting him out of all reason. He was scarlet to the ears. One would think, said Susan to herself, that I was the one who'd been taking liberties. He really is a bit of an ass.

'You're not angry, are you? I'm sorry, I'd no right to do that.'

'No, *I'm* not angry.' She took one light step towards him, put her arm calmly about his neck, and drew his head down to her, kissing him firmly on the mouth. 'Are *you*?' His helpless astonishment might almost be considered a provocation, she thought as she released him. 'I'm going up to bed now,' she said cheerfully. 'Do you think you'll need any help with Richard?'

Laurence shook his head, swallowed hard, but remained speechless.

'Good night, then! Happy Christmas!'

She was halfway up the stairs before he managed to get out a stunned and breathless: 'Good night!'

In a daze he opened the door of the terrace room, and stepped into the glimmer of snowlight and lamplight within. The old man at the table in the window did not move. Laurence crossed the room to him very quietly, unwilling to disturb him too roughly. There was something about the midnight silence of the house that made him tread softly and hold his breath. The burning flush was still on his cheeks as he bent over Richard, and more than half his mind was still with Susan Conroy when he laid his hand gently on the old man's thin shoulder.

'Mr Hellier—'

Richard bowed forward from the delicate touch, his weight collapsing slowly to the right as he fell. His forearm, sliding across the table, knocked over the empty liqueur glass and sent it rolling away towards the far edge. Laurence shot out his left hand instinctively to field it before it fell to the floor, and set it upright again with trembling fingers. His right arm was locked about the old man. He sank to his knees beside him, hoisting his weight back into the chair.

'Mr Hellier, wake up— Richard—!' His voice cracked absurdly, he heard the breath whistling between his lips. The old man's arms rolled stiffly into his lap, his head lolled helplessly over the back of the chair. In the worn face, bluish and cold under the frosty night, the eyes stared half-open. No voice in this world, no touch of a living hand, was ever going to disturb Richard's sleep again.

CHAPTER V

*And who asked you to meddle, in the name
of mischief?*

Act 3

Laurence went up the stairs three at a time, and
hammered at the doctor's door. A startled voice,
thick with sleep, demanded irritably what the devil
was going on, but before the words had disentangled
themselves Laurence was across the room and on his
knees by the bed, shaking at a hunched shoulder, and
panting into the doctor's ear: 'Come down, quickly!
Something's happened to Richard.'

'What are you burbling about, boy?' grunted the
doctor. 'He's next door. If he wanted me he'd call
me.'

'He isn't next door, he's downstairs, and there's
something desperately wrong with him. I think he's
dead.'

'Dead!' The word brought Dr Randall out of bed
in one leap. He reached for his dressing gown, pushing Laurence before him towards the door. 'You're
probably tight or off your head, lad, but we'll soon
see. Where is he?'

'In the little room opposite the bar, where he's
been most of the evening. I just came in. The light
was still on – I thought he'd dropped off to sleep—'

'He was all right about ten, I spoke to him then myself.'

'Well, he isn't now. I can't wake him. I'm sure he isn't breathing. When I touched him he fell over.'

The draught from the open window blew the door to on their heels with a slam. At the top of the stairs Neil stood knotting the cord of his dressing gown about him. 'What on earth's going on? Is something the matter?'

'We don't know yet,' snapped the doctor, and plunged down the stairs without more words. Down they went on his heels, and behind them they heard other doors opening, other voices sleepily and irritably enquiring what all the noise was about. Soon they would all be trailing anxiously downstairs to see for themselves; none of them would consent to be left out of anything, even sudden death.

'What's happened?' Neil was plucking at Laurence's sleeve as they reached the hall. 'Somebody ill? Who—?' He saw the pool of light spilling through the open doorway, and the frail body collapsed into itself in the chair by the window. 'Hellier! My God, what's he done?'

The air was full of questions, upstairs and down, spoken and unspoken, and no one was answering them. The doctor swung a chair from the next table and sat down beside the old man's body, clasped the thin wrist for a moment, and stiffened perceptibly at the feel of the chilling skin under his fingers.

'Give me some more light, Neil, and get out of my way.' He bent over the body, tilting the head gently back upon his arm, and the half-veiled eyes stared unmoving into the glare of the lamps. They waited, holding their breath, and the others, crowding in after them with anxious enquiries, saw the motionless face bathed in light, and fell silent in their turn. Susan was there, still fully dressed, Miranda wrapped in a brushed nylon housecoat, Trevor with his shock of grey hair on end, and a scarf tucked into the neck of his dressing gown. Last and largest, McHugh filled the doorway, yawning.

'What's going on here, for Pete's sake?'

He saw Richard's body, and his jaw dropped. He stood gaping in consternation, clutching at the back of a chair. No one spoke until the doctor lowered the heavy head gently, and pressed down the half-raised eyelids.

'Dead?' said Neil in a whisper.

'Quite dead. Been dead round about half an hour, I should judge.'

'But how? What was it, heart?'

'Hypnotic poisoning,' said the doctor succinctly. 'Almost certainly morphine. Most probably taken in the brandy.'

The momentary hush was absolute, and closed on their hearts like iron. Then Trevor asked hoarsely: 'But for God's sake, why should he want to kill himself?'

'We don't know that he did,' said the doctor in the direst of voices. 'I said he died of hypnotic poisoning, probably morphine. I didn't say he took it wilfully. If I'm right about the morphine, it doesn't take too much thought to discover where it came from.' He looked round at all the blanched faces, and selected Neil as the most detached and responsible person present. 'Will you come up with me and see? I'd prefer to have a witness.'

'Your drugs should be locked up,' said Trevor bluntly.

'My drugs were locked up. If someone has got hold of morphine from my bag – Richard or anyone else – it was not through any negligence, believe me.' His voice was grim. He looked again at Neil.

'Yes,' said Neil, 'you're right. No one had better be alone for the time being. I don't know if you've thought yet of implications, all of you, but if you don't mind, I think it would be better if you all stay here together while we go upstairs.'

They stayed, silent and unmoving, hardly breathing. The doctor passed between them and climbed the stairs, Neil at his back.

'Was your room locked during the day, while you weren't in it?' asked Neil in a low voice.

'No, but my bag was in the wardrobe, and both bag and wardrobe were locked. Though I suppose all the wardrobes have similar keys.'

'Do you always carry morphine?'

'Not always. But one of my last visits was to a patient with cardiac asthma. I had some tablets in my bag for him, though in the end I didn't use them, he was coming out of it very well.'

The unpainted wardrobe was still locked. But when the doctor turned the key and lifted out the black leather case, he saw at once that it had been slit open along the frame with a sharp knife. The cut was clean, even the edges of the silk lining unfrayed. He passed his hand through the slit, and found it large enough to let him feel his way carefully through the contents.

'Well, is there something missing?' asked Neil, moistening his lips.

The doctor unlocked the case, and went through it methodically, item by item. Neil put out a hand to help him, and he frowned it away warningly. 'I shouldn't. No need to complicate things.'

'No,' said Neil, paling, 'you're right.' He stood for a moment staring at the array of tubes, bottles, and instruments. 'But *who* could have done it?'

'Any one of us. Even I myself, I suppose,' said the doctor with a twisted smile, 'if I intended to make that particular use of what I took out of here.' He began to put back the things he had removed. 'All right, that's it. I had a tube of quarter-grain papaveretum tablets, ten of them. It's a compound of the hydrochlorides of alkaloids of opium, largely morphine. They're gone.' He locked the case again, and then laughed mirthlessly at the useless precaution. 'We'll leave this here. The less any of the relevant items are touched, the better. One of us has got to explain to those people down there exactly what this implies. And in the circumstances, Neil, I think it had better be you.'

'What difference does it make?' said Neil. 'We're all in it, every one of us. All right, I'll tell them. If they haven't already worked it out for themselves.'

The company in the terrace room had hardly moved. Miranda was sitting on the edge of a chair, a handkerchief at her eyes; she knew what was due to death, even so inexplicable and ominous a death as this. The others were still standing in a close little huddle near to Richard's body, and their eyes left it only to fix upon the doctor and Neil as they entered the room.

'A phial of tablets containing morphine has been taken from the doctor's bag,' said Neil in a flat voice.

61

'It would appear that some of those tablets killed Richard. The bag was slit open to get them. You must all see how serious this is for every one of us. This death was certainly no accident—'

'He could have done it himself,' said Trevor, too strenuously for conviction.

'He could, it's a possibility. But there are others. Richard had just come into possession of a great deal of money. If he hasn't left a will – I'm not his solicitor, so I can't tell you whether he has or not – then five of us here stand to gain very substantially by his death, as you won't have forgotten. Also, only about three hours ago some very indignant things were said about the injustice of his inheriting from Mrs Byrne. I'm not making insinuations, I'm just outlining facts, and we'd all better face them. You must understand that I shall have to give the police a full account of all that's happened today, including the contents of Mrs Byrne's will.'

'Police!' Something like a bark of laughter came out of Trevor's lips. 'Don't be a fool! As far as we're concerned the police don't exist until the wind changes. You know as well as we do the village is completely cut off.'

There was a moment of appalled silence. Neil said at last in a shaken voice: 'Believe it or not, I'd forgotten. It begins to look as if someone's been counting on that. Well, that mustn't be allowed to prevent investigation into Richard's death. If the police can't get to us and take the affair out of our hands, we shall have to take care of it ourselves, that's all. Every one of us here must have relevant information. Every one of us will have to account for his movements tonight.'

'I know one thing that's relevant enough.' McHugh hunched a large shoulder against the wall. 'You said a minute ago you didn't know whether Hellier left a will. Fact is, he should have done, but I don't see it around. He was making a will this evening. He asked me to be a witness.'

'*What?*' gasped Neil. His eyes flew to the table on which Richard's right hand still dangled. There was no sheet of paper there, but there was certainly a fountain pen lying on the extreme edge of the table, knocked there, perhaps, when the body fell forward. 'There's no sign of any will here.'

'There was none when I found him,' said Laurence, 'but he *had* been writing. And the pen's still there.'

'I'm telling you, he was making a will. He told me so himself.' McHugh repeated his story briefly and forcibly. He was fully awake now; a little more excitement, and he would begin to enjoy himself. 'That's what he told me. Said at any rate he'd make sure nobody cherished any hopes of his dying intestate. His very words! But he never called me to witness his signature, so it looks as if he never finished the job.'

'For a compelling reason,' said the doctor.

'And five of us here,' Trevor reminded them hollowly, 'stood to gain something like sixty thousand apiece if Richard died before he completed that will.'

Nobody questioned his figures. As he himself had said, he had good reason to know the extent of Antonia's fortune, it was he who had conserved and enlarged it for her. They stood silent, avoiding one another's eyes.

'There may still be a previous will in existence,' said the doctor at last.

'There may. But the very fact of his beginning to make one on the spot, and what he said to McHugh here, suggests that there isn't. That's certainly what it would suggest to anyone who found him at it.'

'But surely,' quavered Miranda, emerging from her handkerchief with startling vigour for one who had just been in decorous tears, 'surely if he was making a will that makes it much more likely that he intended to commit suicide?'

'It might have,' said the doctor, 'if he'd finished the job. But you see he didn't. Even if he'd miscalculated the speed with which the stuff would take effect, and been overcome before he could finish his writing, the will would be here to be seen. It isn't. No, someone else was behind this death, I'm afraid, someone who made away with the will as well as the man.'

'One of us,' said Susan in a very low voice.

'Not necessarily. But that's one of the most obvious possibilities.' Neil stood frowning at the floor, the fingers of one hand locked nervously in the thick hair at his temple. 'I'm trying to think what we ought to do. We shan't be cut off for ever, maybe it won't even last many days. But in the meantime there's no one here with authority, we can rely only on ourselves. What I'm suggesting is that we must voluntarily do for ourselves what the police would take off our hands if they could be here. Everyone must make a written statement of his movements tonight, with times as far as possible. The doctor must make a medical report. We must photograph everything that might be relevant. All this evidence, everything we can compile, we must hold at the disposal of the police when we can get in touch. Are you all willing to co-operate?'

The subdued but vehement murmur of agreement was broken by Trevor's sour bark of laughter. There was no need to question or explain it this time. No one was likely to admit to feeling unco-operative; to stand aside, even to show reluctance, was to draw attention to oneself as the man who had something to hide. Yes, they would all sit down earnestly and work out their little timetables, with their eyes on one another, wondering if so-and-so could be relied on to back up this statement, or somebody else to confirm a guessed-at time. There would be an armed truce, deceptively dutiful and responsible. The claws would show again only when someone began to feel himself edged into a corner.

'Couldn't we at least move into the dining room?' asked Susan quietly. 'There isn't anything we can do for Richard, I know, but— We're facing the probable fact that one of us killed him. It hardly seems decent, somehow, to talk like this across his body.'

'Yes, we will move. And as soon as the doctor's finished with him, and we've taken photographs, we'll take him away from here. The Mehlerts will surely be home soon, we shall have to ask for statements from them, too. In the meantime, none of us must be alone.' They did not ask why, they already understood. 'Trevor, I think you've got your camera with you. Have you got flash equipment?'

'Yes, enough for the job.'

'Then will you go up and get whatever you need? Laurence, will you go with him? Doctor, if you want to make a more detailed examination, perhaps it could wait until Trevor's finished? Unless half an hour or so matters?'

'I can do more when I can move him,' said the doctor.

'Right, then when they come down with the camera will you stay here with Trevor while he does his job? The rest of us will go into the dining room and write our statements. We must stay together until the Mehlerts come. We need someone who's—' He hesitated, wincing.

'In the clear,' the doctor supplied bitterly.

'Less involved than we are, at any rate.'

'There's one more thing we could be doing,' volunteered McHugh, his eyes now kindling with an interest which was already warming into enjoyment. 'With talcum powder and a lot of patience we could have a shot at bringing up all the fingerprints. There's nothing to it. The results won't be as efficient as with police methods, but by the time they get here there'll be nothing left of the evidence. I'll have a look in the office, if you like, and find an ink pad and some paper, and get everybody's prints recorded.'

Neil looked back at him speechlessly; the eruption of genuine enthusiasm in this crisis had taken his breath away.

'Or better still,' pursued McHugh, steadily brightening in the glow of his own ingenuity, 'if there's any glossy black paper we could record the prints in talcum powder, too. Shiny black carbon paper would do perfectly. Makes it easier for purposes of comparison, having both lots brought up in white. I'll go and see what I can find, if the office isn't locked.'

'All right, what can we lose? As you say, the police

aren't here to do the job properly. Better an incomplete record than none. I'll come with you. Mrs Quayne and Susan, if you'd like to move into the dining room we'll come back to you there.'

The animals went in two by two, thought Susan, as they complied. I watch you, Miranda, and you watch me, to make sure that neither of us opens a window unobserved, and tosses a little phial out into the snow. Laurence keeps an eye on Trevor upstairs, to make sure he collects only his camera and equipment. Neil walks round the office on McHugh's heels – as a matter of form, I suppose, for what on earth can McHugh have to do with Richard's death? Of all people here, he had nothing to gain, he didn't even know him, except as one of his passengers. Still, Neil was right, everyone must be treated alike until it became clear who had had opportunity, as well as motive. And the Mehlerts – what exactly did he want with them? Yes, of course, foolish of her not to have realised. When everyone had surrendered his fingerprints and made a clean breast of his movements – or in the case of the hypothetical 'he' submitted an edited version – there remained certain necessary formalities, after which those who still believed they would be able to sleep might be allowed to go to bed and try. A search of persons, and a search of belongings. For that they needed Franz and his wife, who, if not 'in the clear', were at least 'less involved than we are'.

Presently Laurence came in and joined them, and hard on his heels came McHugh and Neil. Office and bathroom between them had supplied everything McHugh demanded: fine talcum, and plenty of carbon sheets of the tissue-thin kind, with a smooth black coating that took prints as clearly as glass. McHugh dabbled his own fingers in the talcum first, flicked off the surplus, and left the impressions of both hands upon the glossy surface. The energetic delight of the technician was in his face, and Richard's death had ceased to disturb him. He looked upon the impressive result of his experiment with almost excessive satisfaction, and labelled it carefully.

'You see? It works. Now, Mrs Quayne, if you wouldn't mind—'

'Mr Everard,' began Miranda in a voice quivering with irritation and strain, 'I do feel that this is going too far. Are you seriously suggesting that *I* may have—'

Laurence put his arm round her shoulders, with resignation rather than tenderness, though his voice was gentle enough as he said: 'Mother, please do as he asks. Not because it's possible you could ever have harmed Richard, but because it's impossible. We're all in this together, and there aren't any privileges, but you know you've nothing to hide, so don't behave as if you have.'

'Well, of course I've nothing to hide! But I agree under protest, Mr Everard, you understand?' She surrendered her hands frigidly to McHugh's attentions, and withdrew from the table again with a look of incredulous distaste. Susan followed her in silence, and Laurence, and Neil. The array of labelled sheets grew, completed at last with the addition of Trevor's and the doctor's, when they came in together from the other room.

'We shall need some samples from the Mehlerts, too,' observed the amateur expert, surveying his work contentedly, 'and even from Agathe in the bar. She served me with the brandies, so I must have hers for purposes of elimination. Mine will be on the glass, naturally. And Dr Randall's will obviously be on his bag. But I'll begin with Mr Hellier's chair and the table, and the glass, if somebody'll come and chaperone me?'

Trevor went out with him.

'I've finished with the body,' said the doctor. 'As soon as Herr Mehlert comes home I think we might move him. I suppose you've thought, Everard, that it will be necessary to go ahead with preparations for burial? No doubt Mehlert will know where to find a coffinmaker in the village.'

All the pens and pencils labouring wearily at time-tables of this appalling Christmas Eve checked for a moment. How terribly easy it was to forget the dead man, as though he alone had no rights and no grievance, and they, sweating here for their own lives, were the injured parties. Susan felt tears start for the first time, so vivid was her sudden recollection of Richard as a living man, intelligent, courtly, old, with a lifetime of song behind him, and a wise, rueful smile that held the sum of his experience in it. She looked quickly across at Laurence; his face was shaded by his hand, and only by his stillness and tension did she know that he had just been brought up short, as she had, against the reality of death.

Quietly and disinterestedly the doctor's voice pursued: 'He died, I should say, approximately between eleven and half past. There's no doubt the dose was dropped into the brandy; there are decided traces of a sediment in the glass. Water would have

provided a better solvent than spirits, but the
murderer probably didn't know that. No, I haven't
touched it, your self-appointed expert won't find any
prints of mine there to confuse the issue. I went up
to bed shortly before ten myself, and he was
certainly alive and conscious then, for the door
happened to be standing open when I came through
the hall, and I said good night to him. Without going
into the room, by the way. And he answered me.'

'Was the glass full or empty then?' asked Neil,
looking up from his writing.

'I'm sorry. I simply didn't notice.'

'How many of the tablets do you suppose were
used?'

'Difficult to tell. Four would have been ample,
probably even three, but of course whoever did it
may have known very little about them, and used
more.'

'So there ought to exist, somewhere, the phial
containing the remainder. Unless, of course, they've
been disposed of already.'

'Somehow,' said the doctor slowly, 'I don't think
they'd be thrown away. Especially having been used
once. Somehow one doesn't lightly part with the
symbols of super-human power. When you've killed
once, the means must always appeal as something
to be retained. How do you know it may not come
in useful again?'

They had all raised their heads, and were staring
silently at him, as though a shaft of prophetic truth
had launched itself out of the chaos and transfixed
them, when they heard from the hall the sudden ring
of steps instantly recognisable as belonging to the
innocent, to people who as yet knew nothing of the

disaster which had invaded their house and poisoned
their festival. Frau Mehlert's soft voice spoke, and
Liesl's young, fresh one answered. The doors
between were closed, and allowed the passage of
sound but not of light. Neil rose from his chair with
reluctance and resignation.

'They're back. I must go and tell them.'

He was gone what seemed a long time. They
strained their ears after the exchanges without, and
quivered to the changes of tone, the passing of the
placidity and joy in which the Mehlerts had come
home, the invading notes of incredulity and horror.
When the door opened again they all braced
themselves. But it was McHugh who came bounding
in, carrying the little liqueur glass carefully in a
handkerchief in his palm. After him came Trevor,
Neil and the three Mehlerts, bewildered and
distressed, shocked into silence. He made straight for
the table where his labelled exhibits were laid out
neatly in a row, and the look of eagerness and
satisfaction on his face was at once ludicrous and
frightening.

'We've got something here, I think. The table and
the back and arms of the chair are a mess, so many
prints there's no chance of disentangling them. But
here it's a different matter. I saw Agathe wash and
polish that glass before she filled it. Well, here, look,
there's my right thumb and what I take to be index
and middle fingers, and here in two places we have
Richard's, the same hand, and here's what I expect
to be Agathe's. All just as you might expect.'

It was impossible not to be drawn into his
excitement, it was so vigorous and so innocent of all
desire to offend. They left their imposed labours, and

71

came crowding round him as he pointed out the powdery marks, some clear and sharp, most blurred and overprinted.

'But here, look, here's a beauty of a left hand – see, here the whole length of the thumb to well below the first joint, and here on the other side three fingertips. Somebody took hold of that glass pretty firmly. Maybe his hand was shaking. And look, it prints clean across mine and Richard's here. It's super-imposed over all the others. Let's see if it matches up with any of ours.'

They were leaning over his shoulders now as he lowered the glass beside print after print of the left hand. Those behind could see nothing, but they craned and peered just the same. Those in front narrowed their eyes anxiously, trying to see as keenly as his borrowed watch-maker's glass enabled him to do.

'Not Mrs Quayne's – not Mr Mason's – not— Yes, we've got it, this is it! Fingers – thumb – no mistake about it.' He jerked up his head, stiffening like a pointer fixing his quarry.

'It's Laurence!' he said.

CHAPTER VI

Is all this scurvy crew
Plotted to do me mischief?

Act 3

'I did that when I came in and found him.' Laurence, alarmed in spite of himself, drew back a step before the assault of so many dilated eyes, and was brought up sharply by the edge of a table. A wave of colour flooded his face from throat to brow; he was infuriated by it, but could not suppress it. Nor did he like the defensive tone of his own voice, rushing onward too precipitately, too anxiously, but he could not subdue it to a reasonable pitch. 'He fell forward when I touched him to wake him up, and his arm knocked it over and it started to roll. I grabbed it to save it from falling to the floor. As soon as I touched him he fell forward. I *told* you!'

'You told us he fell, yes,' said the doctor reasonably. 'You didn't say anything about the glass.'

'I didn't even think about it. I just grabbed it and put it back on the table. I had my hands full with him.'

'All right, all right!' said McHugh soothingly. 'Nobody's accusing you. All I say is, there's the print of your left hand.'

'And of your right. And that's a good deal more

significant, if you'll think for a moment.' He knew he was being a fool, but he couldn't stop. There *had* been an accusation in the presentation of this simple, accidental fact, and every person present there had sensed it, and he was damned if he was going to take it lying down. 'Who gave him the drink? You did. Who had a better opportunity to doctor it than you?'

'Oh, come off it, boy,' said McHugh tolerantly. 'At least a dozen people in the bar saw me take two glasses of brandy from Agathe, and set off across the hall with one in either hand. I went straight to the old boy's table and put his down there for him, and said "Cheers" and came away again. What do you suggest I used to drop the tablets in, one of my feet? And anyhow, why on earth should I want to kill him? *I'm* not one of the lucky legatees. But there's no reason to go off at half-cock at the first bit of evidence that turns up.'

'Anyhow,' persisted Laurence, trying hard to master his nerves and his voice, 'prints on the glass don't prove a thing. It wasn't necessary to handle it in order to drop some tablets into it. You must see that. Anyone could have done it if Richard's attention was deflected for a minute. It probably stood there a good while, because he was still drinking his beer. A dozen people might have looked in to have a word with him before he drank the cognac. In any case Richard was dead by the time *I* touched the glass. That was the only time I approached him alone the whole evening. Susan was with me all the time until we came in just before midnight, and saw him still sitting there.' He wished to God she'd stayed with him while he went to awaken the sleeper, but at least she could and would vouch for the way he had spent his evening.

He drew a deep steadying breath, and turned confidently to Susan. The look in her eyes shook him to the heart. He clutched at the table behind him and held his breath. Why was she staring at him like that?

'You *did* go and speak to Richard for a few minutes,' he heard her saying in a faint, frightened voice, and the words seemed to come from an appalling distance. 'Before we went out – about half past nine it must have been – Mr McHugh had only just come out and left the brandy there on the table. You can't have forgotten. You asked me to wait for you.'

'But I never went out of your sight!' gasped Laurence. He couldn't believe in this, it wasn't happening. 'You were there in the doorway the whole time, you must have seen every move I made.'

She stared back at him with dark eyes enormous in a blanched face, but she stood her ground. 'You were between me and the table,' she said. 'I couldn't see the glass while you were standing there – or your hands. You *could* have—'

'But it was only a matter of seconds.' He could hardly speak, the breath had gone out of him as though he had been hit hard in the solar plexus. 'And how could I have got hold of the morphine? You'd been with me all the time in the bar—' His voice foundered in the shoals of sand in his throat, and ceased to make any sound.

'I'm sorry, but I can't tell anything but the truth, how can I? You'd just been upstairs to get your coat – and the doctor wasn't in his room then, he was still in the dining room, I heard his voice while I was waiting for you to come down. Laurence, you must see I have to tell the truth – I can't help it!' She was almost in tears, but that didn't alter the things she was saying. 'You *could* have taken the tablets then – and you *could* have used them!'

Laurence felt behind him very carefully for a chair, dragged it round towards him, and let himself down dizzily into it. Miranda uttered a strangling sob and made a darting move towards him, and then, changing course as though a gale had blown her aside, turned and went for Susan like a fury, her fingers crooked into claws.

'You bitch!' shrieked the prim, pale mouth, contorted viciously. 'You murderous, lying bitch!' No one had ever heard such words from her before; the epithet most of them would have been prepared to swear was totally unknown to her, but she gave it the force of a slingshot. 'I'll kill you,' she raved, 'I'll kill you for this!'

The attack was so unexpected that Susan threw up her hands and the men sprang between them far too late. The nails of Miranda's right hand clawed red weals down Susan's cheek, the left hand locked hard fingers in her hair. She gripped at a bony wrist, and fended off the second slash by a matter of an inch or so, forcing the lean hand violently away from her face. The one cry she had uttered under the shock of the assault was quite lost under the flood of Miranda's frenzied screams.

Then Trevor and the doctor had flung themselves between the two women, and Neil had Miranda by the left wrist and was trying to prise open the fingers locked in Susan's hair. It took them all their time to drag the two apart without damage. Miranda fought like an infuriated cat, writhing so violently that they could hardly hold her, and shrieking all the time on a wildly rising scale that was physical pain in the ears. No words now, only an agonising, hysterical screaming. When her strength failed her she collapsed through their arms to the floor, and lay cackling and howling in demented grief and laughter, and flinging herself about so recklessly at every approach that they were afraid to touch her.

The doctor pushed Laurence brusquely aside, dropped to his knees beside her, and held her down by the shoulders. Without turning his head he ordered urgently: 'Neil, fetch my bag!' Neil was already at the door when he added sharply: 'Don't handle it!'

'Right!' Neil shouted back, and fled up the stairs three at a time.

'Frau Mehlert, some water!'

Frau Mehlert ran, too. Her husband brought a cushion for Miranda's head. Liesl stood motionless by the door, saying nothing and missing nothing. She was nineteen, large, calm and rather beautiful. She had never seen hysterics before, and possibly never would again, and she was natural enough to be fascinated by the exotic. Laurence stood wavering helplessly between Susan's dishevelled hair and bleeding face and his mother's infinitely more distressing collapse. He knew he could do nothing, and yet did not feel absolved from trying. And all the while, hoarsely now, with a note of exhaustion in her shrillness, Miranda screamed.

The doctor was sparing of words and movements as he was of drugs, and even the shock of cold water he employed sparingly and neatly. The monotonous screams halted in a sharp gasp at the first tilt of the pitcher, then resumed feebly and spasmodically. At the second they subsided, and then faded naturally into quiet and exhausted weeping. Miranda lay open-eyed, limp, and pathetic. Frau Mehlert went on her knees beside her and dried her face with smooth, round movements of a calm hand. Disturbances of a kind so easily comprehensible restored her large tranquillity.

'That's better,' said the doctor shortly. 'Now be quiet and lie still.' Neil was at his elbow, the bag carried carefully by its handle in a folded handkerchief, but the doctor took it firmly in his hands and opened it on the floor beside him. His prints would be all over it in any case, why should he fight shy of a few extra ones now? 'Get me a glass, please.' He gave her a sedative, and supported her while she swallowed it docilely. 'We'd better get her to bed at once. Frau Mehlert, will you help me with her?'

Miranda's convulsive trembling was ebbing now, and her strength seemed to have gone with it. She was so weak that they almost had to lift her to her feet and carry her upstairs. Laurence started forward to help her, but Neil took him by the wrist, quite gently, and held him back.

'Not you, Laurence, if you don't mind. Randall and Frau Mehlert will take good care of her, they don't need you.'

He understood only too well, but he made no complaint. He followed his mother's lame departure with sombre eyes, and said nothing. The trio were already in the hall when Neil released his hold, and went quickly after them. 'Frau Mehlert, please—' He followed them to the foot of the stairs, and the murmur of low voices went on for a few moments.

Those in the dining room caught little of what passed, but Frau Mehlert's full, warm voice illuminated their darkness, enquiring without astonishment: 'And for what must I look?'

Neil came back into the room and closed the door. 'I've asked Frau Mehlert to examine Mrs Quayne's belongings. I hope you'll all understand that we've no alternative. We have to try and find that phial with the remaining tablets, and the only fair way is to submit to a general search. If anyone wants to object, do it now.'

No one objected, and now not even Trevor found the heart to laugh. McHugh said: 'The sooner the better. After that's been done I take it we needn't follow one another about any more, and we might even snatch a couple of hours sleep.'

'Yes, I think we might. We shall have done all we can do at the moment. I shall ask Franz here to go through what pockets we've got among us in this rig, and then to look through our rooms. And Liesl will go upstairs with you, Susan.' He approached her solicitously; she was sitting silent, withdrawn from the light; on her left cheek the four weals had bled a little and dried into dark-red lines. She looked beyond him to where Laurence stood, and her eyes were dilated and dark.

'Are you all right, Susan? I'm terribly sorry about this. You mustn't blame yourself, you couldn't do anything else.'

'I'm all right,' she said steadily, and rose from her chair. 'I'll go.' But from the door she looked back, and took a step towards Laurence, putting out an almost pleading hand.

'Laurence, you must understand—'

79

'I do understand,' he said curtly, and turned his back on her.

She put her hands to her face, and turned and went out blindly, and Liesl put an arm round her shoulders and led her away. Laurence stood rigid until he heard the door close behind them, then he shrugged his way violently out of his coat, and began to empty his pockets upon one of the tables.

'Better begin with me. I'm the only one still dressed. I suppose that's a suspicious circumstance, too.'

'There's no need to take it like that.' Neil was getting irritable with weariness, it showed in the abruptness of his movements and the arduous quietness and reasonableness of his voice. 'We all propose to go through the same process, it makes no difference who's first. Stop behaving as though you've been charged with murder.'

'There you are, feel for yourself.' Laurence raised his arms, and turned about defiantly under Franz Mehlert's searching hands. 'Satisfied? May I pocket my things again?' He sat straight and watchful while they all in turn submitted to the same examination, but nothing illicit was turned out upon the table.

'Maybe we should begin upstairs by looking in Mr Hellier's room,' suggested McHugh then, 'in case it's been disturbed in any way, or anything taken from it.'

No one believed in the possibility of discovering anything by that means, but it was their obvious duty to look. They went upstairs in a body, all five of them, but there was a subtle difference now in the way they clung together. They had begun this horrible night with everyone looking sidelong at everyone else. Now Laurence moved in the middle of them with a hectic colour burning in his face and his eyes fixed before him, while they watched him covertly from all sides, and evaded his eyes as often as he turned his head. He knew it, and could not even defend himself; they would only find additional evidence in his very sensitivity to looks and words.

At the top of the stairs they encountered Susan and Liesl, newly emerged from Susan's bedroom; they had heard a door close as they mounted to the turn of the staircase. The two girls were flushed but calm. Susan had changed into pyjamas and housecoat.

'We have finished,' said Liesl, in the careful English of which she was both proud and shy. 'There is nothing.'

'Thank you,' said Neil. 'And Mrs Quayne?'

'There also not. My mother and the doctor are still with the lady, but soon I think she sleeps.'

'Good! If you don't mind helping us for a little longer, I should like you to be with us while your father looks in our rooms, too. It's best that we should all be witnesses.'

Richard's room, empty and orderly, presented no revelations. His suitcases were disposed neatly on the luggage stand, but they were empty. He had unpacked, and arranged his clothes meticulously in the wardrobe. His briefcase, which seemed to be exactly as on arrival, lay on one of the shelves, unlocked but fastened, and its contents were what might have been expected, his personal papers, a flat writing case containing some letters, a travel book with the flap of the dust jacket turned in to keep his place, a wallet of photographs from Antonia's last tour, and some notices cut from the newspapers of several countries. There was also a small and not very good miniature of Antonia as a girl, painted on ivory, in a worn leather case.

'So that's what he wouldn't leave behind in the plane,' said McHugh. 'Well, everything seems in order here. Where next?'

'You'd better begin with me,' said Laurence, jutting his chin aggressively. 'It's what you're all waiting for, why postpone it?'

Neil passed a hand over his forehead in a gesture of sudden disgust and sadness, but acquiesced simply: 'You or another, what difference does it make?'

Laurence had the small room at the end of the wing that enclosed the farmyard. A faint smell of cattle pervaded it; some of the stalls were certainly below. The double window was small, and had no balcony outside; probably the room was usually one of the last to be filled. He threw open the door and stood back to let them go in before him; the little space seemed full to overflowing when they were all inside. He sat down defiantly on the edge of the bed, and drew his feet under him out of their way.

'It's all yours. Anything compromising you can find, I'll eat.'

Neil looked at Franz, who gave a deprecating heave of his shoulders, and went methodically to work, emptying first the wardrobe, then the large suitcase on the luggage stand. Laurence was less tidy with his possessions than Richard had been, and much of his clothing came out of Franz's hands more neatly folded than it had been before. The case provided a great deal of sheet music and some manuscript notes, and the normal assets of a young man who was not particularly interested in his person, but compelled to conform to a certain standard by his share in the public appearances of a celebrity. Indignant hazel eyes, under a fall of disordered fair hair, followed every movement, watched every item taken up or laid down. He hugged his knees and shivered a little. Franz ran his large fingers delicately round the lining of the case, and the angry eyes followed faithfully and bitterly.

The drawers of the dressing table, the shelf over the washbasin, the open brush case, produced nothing that was not expected and approved. There was a book lying on the bedside cabinet, and a large china ashtray beside it, with a tight twist of burned paper lying curled in it. Franz passed both with only a thoughtful glance, and looked round the room to see if he had missed anything.

McHugh, inexhaustible and irrepressible, advanced from among the silent watchers and peered at the ashtray thoughtfully. 'I thought you didn't smoke.'

'I don't.' Laurence turned his head with a jerk to see to what the obscure remark referred, and stiffened and frowned at sight of the coil of black ash, one end ground to powder, the other still intact. There was even a wisp of scorched but unburned paper, by which it had evidently been held between somebody's fingers. But not his. He had not been into his room since fetching his coat, and there had been no such relic in the ashtray then. He straightened on the edge of the bed, and his hands went down and clenched nervously on the yielding softness of the feather quilt. McHugh had picked up the ashtray and was carrying it under the light. With a careful forefinger he probed at the blackened folds to which the scraps of white still adhered.

Franz stretched down a negligent hand and turned back the pillow. A thick black leather notebook, fastened with a metal clasp, lay on the smooth, glazed sheet. He took it up, hesitating whether to open it.

'You can bloody well put that back,' said Laurence, bristling. 'That's my diary.'

'Oh, for God's sake!' yelled Neil in an ungovernable spurt of nerves. 'Nobody's going to interfere with your diary.'

In the act of replacing the book Franz hesitated again, and then slowly drew back his hand. The shape of the soft leather spine was oddly distorted for half its length. It was not obvious to the eye, but his fingers had chafed at the feel of the spot where the bulge ended. He looked once at Laurence, and then snapped open the clasp.

'Put it back, I said.' Laurence came to his feet, raging, but Trevor caught at his arms and held him still. The doctor had entered the room and joined them unobserved, and was watching from just within the doorway. At his shoulder appeared the tired face of Frau Mehlert.

Franz opened the notebook in the middle, so that the pull on the spine was eased. He turned the open book upright and shook it, but whatever was lodged fitted too tightly to slide out upon the bed. He took a pencil from his pocket, and thrust it down the spine, and something moved unevenly before it, and stuck, and moved again.

Laurence had frozen into stupefied stillness now, and was staring with wide eyes at the reluctantly moving bulge which should not have been there. He moistened his dry lips, and tried to speak and could not, as Franz levered out on to the pillow a short tube of glass, stoppered with white plastic, with a hand-written label.

Among the huddle of silent watchers someone heaved a gasping sigh. The doctor stepped forward and fixed upon the phial a long, grim stare; there was no need for him to identify it.

'Only two left,' he said, and looked up into Laurence's blanched face. 'What have you done with the rest of them?'

'I never had them.' Laurence's voice was flat and hopeless; he did not expect to be believed now, whoever had done this to him had managed it only too well. 'I don't know how it got there. I only know I didn't put it there. I never saw it before.'

'Did you use all the rest on Richard?' pursued the doctor relentlessly.

'I tell you I never had them. I know nothing about them.' He closed his eyes for a moment, shaking his head helplessly, trying to rouse himself out of this hideous dream, but when he opened his eyes again the glass phial still lay there upon his pillow. He could not blink it away. 'You don't believe me,' he said without emphasis, 'I know that. But I'm telling you the truth. Someone else has planted the thing on me. Someone's elected me as a scapegoat for this business.'

He raised his head with sudden purpose, and looked for Susan. She stood with her shoulders flattened back against the wall, and her face was as pale and blank as his own. Above the whiteness of her unscarred cheek her eyes looked quite black.

'It's for you I'm carrying the can, isn't it?' he said in an almost inaudible voice. 'I don't know how you did it, but you made a good job of fixing me.'

The great eyes stared back at him, but she made never a sound. It was Neil who said sharply: 'You're wasting your efforts, Laurence. Since you gave the alarm and we all came down Susan hasn't been alone for a moment. She's had no opportunity whatever of planting evidence in your room, and you know it.'

'I know it was done, by her or by someone else. I know I never saw your damned tablets, or that phial, or—'

'Or this?' said McHugh.

He extended the ashtray in one hand. In the other he held a nail file he had picked up from the dressing table. With the point he had prised apart the tatters of scorched paper, and pressed out a thin, frayed ribbon of singed white on which distinct traces of handwritten words showed.

'You need the glass to see it properly, but my sight's above average, and I can tell you now what you'll find there. This bit comes from where one fold was made, it's the end he held when he burned it, and because it was pinched tight it didn't quite burn away. I'm pretty sure the handwriting could be identified by anyone who knows it well, but even without that the few words left are enough.'

He held the ashtray up to Neil's face, and with the tip of the file traced along the faint lines of ink letter by letter. 'Here's only part of a word to start with, but it's clear what it was. "—stament of me, Richa—" And then a bit that's cracked through, and then "—lier, of Silmin—" The name of his house in Dorset is Silmington, isn't it? This is all that's left of Hellier's last will and testament. The one he wasn't allowed to finish. The one I was to have witnessed – if he'd lived long enough to sign it.'

CHAPTER VII

*In this one hour, by heaven, I do
Penance for all my sins!*

Act 2

There was nothing left to him now, no refuge in
anger, or argument, or even surprise, no point in
speaking at all, since he could say only one
inadequate and unconvincing thing over and over,
and that they were never going to believe. He sat
down again slowly on his bed, and clutched his head
between his hands, and stared blankly ahead into a
frozen loneliness, as though they had already left the
room and locked the door upon him.

'Well?' prompted Neil gently, when the silence had
begun to vibrate like a bowstring.

'I know nothing about it. I didn't burn it. I didn't
put it there.' His lips moved stiffly, and the voice that
came out of them had the mechanical intonation of
hypnosis.

Braced back against the wall, Susan stood clinging
with fingers and shoulders and rigid spine to hold
herself upright. She looked as if she might faint.
Why? Wasn't this what she'd been aiming at all
along?

'I think you should satisfy yourself of the genuineness of the evidence. That's only fair.' Astonishing

how patient, how solicitous they could be when they were sure of their man. He was the scapegoat, all right, and holy. He lifted the load from every one of them, the innocent as well as the guilty. Now that they were free of fear for themselves, they could afford to be wonderfully kind to him.

They put the ashtray on his knees, carefully avoiding draughts that might have fanned the fragile shreds apart. They brought the watchmaker's glass and put it into his hand, and with soft encouragement, as to a rebellious child, coaxed him to read the fragmentary words for himself and admit their significance. They brought Richard's engagement book and held it before him so that he could compare the handwriting, and see for himself that there was no deception. And there was none; he wasn't trying to assert that this scrap of paper was not what they claimed for it. They even brought him a stiff drink, and heaven knew he needed it.

'It does appear to be the sheet of notepaper he borrowed tonight to make a will, doesn't it? You'll agree to that?'

'Yes. But I know nothing about it. I never touched it.'

'And it is his handwriting. You're satisfied about that?'

'It seems to be. But I don't know how it got here. I didn't bring it.' The schnapps had brought up two hectic rings of colour on his cheekbones, startling against his pallor. He looked like Petrouchka distraught; even that straw-coloured hair of his fitted into the picture.

'Better tell us about it, Laurence. No need to make bad even worse. What have you done with the rest of the tablets? Or did you use them all?'

'I haven't seen them. I never saw the phial until now. I tell you I know nothing about all this. Someone's planted the things on me.'

'That's hardly reasonable. You know yourself that ever since you roused the doctor we've taken every precaution. We've operated in twos, and nobody's been alone for more than a matter of seconds. No, a frame-up is hardly the most likely explanation of all these damning facts that are piling up against you, you know. There's a much simpler one.'

There was, and they were happy with it, because it lifted the weight from them.

'The phial was well hidden. If Franz hadn't handled the book, but only looked at it, it would never have been spotted.'

'I've told you I know nothing about it, I didn't touch the tablets, I didn't kill Richard. There's nothing else I can say.' And he was sick to death of saying that, he wouldn't repeat it again. What was the use?

'Very well,' said Neil, with a heavy sigh. 'That's how it will have to stand. We shall test the phial for prints, too, but I don't suppose that will add much to what we know.' He was deeply troubled by the blank hopelessness of the pale face before him, stained with those clownish scarlet discs on the cheeks; and on impulse he sat down beside Laurence and laid his hand on the taut fist clenched on the young man's knees. 'Listen to me, Laurence. You yourself must see that in the circumstances there's nothing we can do except hold both you and the evidence until we can hand over this case to the police. All the relevant material, the glass, this tube, that stuff in the ashtray, and all our personal statements will go into Herr Mehlert's safe. And you'll have to stay here in your room, under lock and key. You understand that? I'm sorry, but we can't take the responsibility for leaving you at liberty. I'll see that you have some exercise, and you can ask for anything you need. But this is murder. We have a duty to hold you safely until the proper authorities can take you off our hands. It will be up to them how they proceed after that.'

'And in the meantime,' said Laurence in a thin, bitter voice, 'the chap who did kill Richard can take his time about covering the rest of his tracks.'

'I didn't say investigations will stop.'

'No, you didn't *say* it.'

Neil rose. His eyes, heavy-lidded with weariness, looked round at all the silent faces that stared in upon them. 'We'd better go,' he said, 'and leave him alone. Maybe tomorrow we can talk more sensibly.' He caught the doctor's eye as they moved obediently towards the door. Laurence heard the whispered query: 'D'you think it's all right to leave him?'

'Yes,' he said loudly, 'it's all right to leave me. I've got no morphine, and I wouldn't make use of it if I had. I'm going to survive, make no mistake about that, if only to see somebody damned for this. Now get out, the lot of you! Get the hell out of my room!'

It was McHugh who remembered to pluck the key from the inner side of the lock and transfer it to the outer. A practical man, McHugh. As long as there was something positive to be done, some expenditure of energy to be experienced and enjoyed, he didn't care whether it was crash-landing a plane in the mountains or playing detectives with carbon paper and magnifying glass on the track of one of his passengers. As though action had for him some intrinsic virtue of its own; good action, bad action, any action, maybe even killing. Except that he was one of the two who had nothing whatever to gain by Richard's death.

The door was closed firmly. Laurence strained his ears, and heard the key turn in the lock. In the sudden quietness sounds carried all too clearly, or else his hearing was sharpened by indignation and fear. The murmur of voices outside came back to him distinctly.

'Oughtn't we to tell his mother?' That was McHugh again, the crisp voice toned down as low as it would go.

And Neil answering, in a muted howl of exasperation: 'Oh, for God's sake, haven't you been busy enough for one night? Let the poor woman sleep!'

That warmed him for a moment, that note of detestation and compassion from Neil; but in the silence after they were all gone he sat on the bed with his head in his hands until he grew cold to the heart. Once he heard slow, laboured footsteps on the stairs and along the main corridor, and knew from the weight and caution of these movements that they were bringing up Richard's body. That made two of them exiled here in the night, islanded from their own kind. He felt nearer to Richard now than to any of the others, even his mother. Thank God she was under a sedative, and she'd sleep. Let the poor woman sleep! He was grateful to Neil for that.

He lay down on the bed, fully dressed as he was, and spread his arms on the pillow, and buried his face between them. The discarded diary slid down into the hollow against his armpit, and settled uncomfortably there, and he had not the strength or the heart to stir himself and push it away. He tried to think, to feel his way back through every detail of the nightmare for the flaw which would let him through to the truth; but he was so sick with misery and so sore with indignation that he was conscious of nothing but his own pain.

It wasn't only the burning sense of injury; there's a lot of injustice in the world, it wasn't his first encounter with it, though it might well turn out to be his last. It wasn't even the pure physical and mental terror he felt for himself, though that was real enough. Fear ought to be illogical when you have done nothing wrong, but who really believes the law invariably arrives at truth? No, worst of all was the sense of betrayal. If it had been left entirely to that eager beaver, McHugh, to snatch the ground from under his feet and bring down the roof on him to bury him, it wouldn't have hurt quite so much, because he would still have had a kind of comfort, and some battered fragments of his own internal security. But that Susan should be the one to stick the knife in his back! Why? *Why?* She couldn't believe she was telling the truth. This was no honest, flustered, damn-fool mistake on her part, she wasn't the kind to mix up her memories or get scared to trust her own senses. She knew what she'd seen. She knew he could not possibly have dropped anything into Richard's glass without her seeing it, and she knew she hadn't seen anything of the kind. Not mistake, but malice. And why, for God's sake? Why should she want to do this awful thing to him? What had he ever done to her? And after this evening! No, yesterday evening, of course, it was already Christmas Day, and not so long before dawn now. After that interlude of peace together, unbearably sweet to remember now, and unbearably bitter, why should she turn on him and betray him like this? He sank his teeth into the back of his hand, but the small localized pain didn't help at all, he hardly felt it.

He must keep his head. He must believe that this array of cooked evidence against him was full of flaws, and that the police, when they managed to get here, would find them and pick the whole edifice to pieces. You can't prove a man a murderer when he isn't one. Or can you? Can you, if desperate enough? He thought back feverishly through the annals of British justice, and had not so far to go before he came up against a case which cast considerable doubts on its infallibility. About Austrian law he knew nothing. Maybe there wasn't any death penalty here. He shrank indignantly from the spark of wretched hope that thought kindled in him, furious to think he might have to be grateful for the outrageous gift of a life which was his by right, take it with the smear of guilt still on it, and be thankful for it.

He began to curse under his breath, pouring out into the pillow all the foulest words he knew, against McHugh, against Richard's murderer, whoever he might be, against Susan, against all of them. His repertory was neither extensive nor impressive, and that didn't ease him, either. He remembered the tracks of his mother's nails like strings of little red beads down Susan's cheek, and shrank with loathing and distaste for everything and everybody, himself included. And in this miserable case he drifted unawares into an exhausted sleep.

He awoke sharply to cold and stiffness, and a small, persistent sound as light as the nibbling of mice. He lay shivering, and listened to it as to something left over from a dream, and after a while his sick senses cleared a little, and he was aware of direction and time, the first, faintest foreshowings of the dawn, the dark radiance of a sky still unexpectedly clear of snow. The little tapping sound went on and on, until it drew his attention to the pale panels of the door. Someone was rapping with a fingernail; it must have gone on for a long time before it penetrated his sleep. He lay silent, staring at thè wood as though he could see through it to the person waiting outside.

Close to the crack of the door a voice breathed: 'Laurence!' He made no move, but it went on and on, tapping and whispering: 'Laurence! Can you hear me? Laurence, are you awake?'

What more did she want? Couldn't she be satisfied with what she'd done, that she must come pestering him with self-justifications, too? Bitterness boiled up into his mouth in a rush of gall, and welled into his eyes like tears. He wanted to keep silence and let her pick at his door all the rest of the night, but the voice became an abominable agony with its tireless, urgent repetition of his name.

'Go away!' he said quietly but aloud.

'Laurence, I must talk to you—'

'You've talked enough. Leave me alone!'

'Only for a moment! Please! I want—'

'I don't. I don't want to talk to you, I don't want to see you. If you don't go away and let me alone I'll rouse the house. If they want me to behave they

94

can damn' well protect me from you, at least.'

'Laurence, please, I beg you—'

He swung his feet to the floor and sat trembling, hating her, hating himself, unable to draw back from the course on which he was already launched like a leaf on a tide.

'Go to hell!' he said in a vicious whisper. 'That's my last word.'

Silence, and then the smallest of sounds outside the door, stealthy sounds that made no sense until he closed his eyes and let all his consciousness pass into the sensitivity of his hearing. Then he saw her clearly. She was standing pressed against the closed door, one hand on the handle, the other flattened against the wood, and her cheek pressed just above the handle. The cheek was wet. It was the left one, with the scratches on it, and she laid it upon the unyielding wood of his door, and let the slow, painful tears well from under her closed eyelids. He heard the faint, rhythmic cachinnations of her breath as she laboured to suppress what otherwise would have been tearing sobs. Then she felt her way lamely along the wall and crept away, and in a little while silence filled the corridor.

Laurence turned and flung himself face down into the pillow, and hugged it to him frantically to stifle the convulsions of responsive grief that passed shuddering upwards from his lungs and knotted agonisingly in his throat. He didn't understand anything, he was hopelessly lost. He hated her, and he was sick with shame at having hurt her. It should have been some consolation to him to hear her cry, and instead it was the final, the insupportable anguish. He choked on the tears her tears had

started out of him, and fell brokenly asleep again
with the horrid taste of self-disgust in his mouth.

CHAPTER VIII

Then hold your peace, withdraw,
And wait in patience till I need your
   evidence.

Act 3

No more snow had fallen in the night. The morning of Christmas Day came in a frosty glitter of sunshine, and the vast undulating masses of white seemed to have condensed and hardened. On the gentle slopes just above the village half a dozen children were out on skis. Little things of three and four went feather-stitching merrily up the hill, empty-handed, disdaining sticks, and came rollicking down again as lightly as leaves. When they fell they fell like flakes of snow, and every bit as serenely. Their voices made a constant babel like little treble cow-bells, a rippling sound that seemed to be an attribute of the air, the day, and the place, an emanation of innocence. The sky at midmorning was coloured like an inverted harebell, and all the shadows in the folded planes of snow were blue.

Susan, coming down very late, met Franz Mehlert in the hall, and he smiled and greeted her with a flashing of white teeth out of the thicket of his beard. She had very little knowledge of German and understood nothing except 'nice weather', but she heard

Ellis Peters

in his voice and saw in his smile the same desire to comfort and sustain she had heard and seen up there on the mountain, when he came looming out of the night and offered them shelter and rest. All distresses fell within the field of his monumental, calm kindness, but some he could help, and some he could not, and he knew no way of distinguishing between them here. These chance visitors, these most unfortunate strays from another world, were so far out of his scope, and so absorbed in themselves, that he knew in his blood and bones that it would be waste of effort trying to understand them. They were only sojourners, they would go away again as soon as they could, having learned nothing. But he could still feel sorry for them. And the girl was pitiful. She had seemed to be a cocksure young person enough when she came, travelled, efficient, a product of the modern secretarial college. She looked like any other distraught young girl now, pale as her white blouse, with the dull red scratches distorting one cheek, and great hollows under her too-brilliant eyes, hollows bluer than the shadows in the snow. Synthetic cataclysms she could probably have dealt with, but the natural immensities, like death and anger and hate, disconcerted and overwhelmed her.

And yet she had a grave and quiet look about her, too, as though she was aware of having changed direction. Perhaps she would learn something, after all, from this bad experience; something about her own identity.

She said: '*Guten Morgen*, Herr Mehlert!' and returned him the ghost of his warming smile, but she could not talk to him. She did not even remember, in her tired condition, the German for 'Merry

98

Christmas', or she would have offered it as a reasonable wish from her to him. In spite of crime and death, in spite of his pity for the dead and the living, it was entirely fitting that he should enjoy the deeper content of the season, and be in no way ashamed of it. But her tongue felt thick and clumsy, and her brain would not work. She went on into the dining room.

Trevor Mason was sitting alone over breakfast, a magazine spread open beside his plate. She sat down opposite him, returning his subdued greeting as disconsolately. It was an ordeal to face any one of her companions this morning, but as well Trevor as any.

'So it didn't snow, after all.'

'No. Mehlert says two or three days of this weather could open the track. They'll probably begin to cut through from this end today, even if it is Christmas Day. But if the wind veers again there may be more snow.' He got up from his chair, and went to look out from the window, drumming nervously on the pane with his long fingers. 'The sooner we get out of here the better. Three days I can just about face, but much longer and I shall be ready for the psychiatrists. If there was even a telephone line working I could stick it.'

Trevor's most urgent need of a telephone line was almost invariably connected with money. She wondered if Laurence had been right in saying that Trevor 'could use a little margin at the moment'. Had he really been hoping for a large windfall from Antonia to tide him over a risky patch? It was not impossible. Once she had heard Antonia scolding him, in a manner almost maternal, for being an incorrigible gambler, and it had seemed to her a strange accusation to make against one who guarded the affairs of his client so scrupulously. But apparently he was less orthodox in handling his own. There was, after all, something of the natural adventurer about him, and he had flirted with danger in every other field. Both his marriages, for instance, doomed from the start but dazzling while they lasted, both contracted with cometlike figures from the most hectic circles of the entertainment world. His three race horses had lost plenty for him, too, as well as bringing him in the occasional big win. No, he hadn't hoarded his own assets as he had Antonia's.

'Where are the others?' she asked, pouring coffee.

'Randall's with Mrs Quayne.' He did not look round, but she saw the lines of his mobile mouth tighten wryly. 'Someone had to tell her about the boy, and – if you'll forgive the observation – we could hardly ask you to do the womanly office, could we? In any case, it was a certainty Randall would be wanted as soon as she heard the worst. She'll be under sedatives again by now, nothing else for it. I don't suppose we shall see her today.'

'She'll want to see him,' said Susan, staring into her cup. At the thought of the meeting between mother and son she shivered. 'And I don't see how they can refuse.'

'Poor devil!' said Trevor,and it was by no means clear which of the two he meant.

'Where's Neil? And Mr McHugh?'

'I don't know. Gone before I got up, apparently. Neil may be through in the kitchen. The undertaker came a little while ago. We don't know how long we may be here, they'll have to coffin him, even if we can't bury him – Oh, God, I'm sorry, Susan!' he said, aghast. 'I could have spared you that over the breakfast table. This business has played hell with my wits.'

'That's all right. It has with all of us. After the fact it would be a bit phony to object to the wording, wouldn't it?'

'And McHugh – I don't know, he must be out somewhere. I've no doubt he came down early and ate a hearty breakfast. He's probably borrowed some boots and skis by now, and is out on the slopes with the kids. He's got to do something with his energy.'

He came back to the table, and stood turning the pages of his magazine. 'Did you see this? I bought it at Schwechat just before we took off, but I never opened it until this morning. There's an obituary. Done in a hurry, but it's good. The pictures must be from the Opera House files, they never came to me for them. Some very fine ones, too.' He lingered over them sombrely, and over the rim of her cup she studied them with him, upside down. The costumes made them all identifiable. There was one of Antonia as Astrofiammante, marvellously royal and sinister, with a coronal of stars, and one, inevitably, as the Marschallin in her third-act splendour, with a waist Susan could have spanned in her two hands, and breasts half-uncovered, and her own hair dressed in a glittering jewelled tower on her head.

'Would you believe,' said Trevor, 'that she was fifty-six when that was taken? Do you know how old Marie Therese was supposed to be? Thirty. And she played that role when she was twenty-two, and she played it when she was sixty, and every time

101

magnificently. There was never another like her,and
now there never will be.'

The hand that held open the magazine moved
gently upon the page, smoothing it with an involuntary gesture of tenderness, as though he touched the
silken whiteness of the exposed breast. His hands
were imaginative and expressive while his face was
elderly and sceptical, but it was the hands she
believed. He must always have been in love with
Antonia, ever since he came to her twenty years ago.
He in his late thirties, with two discarded wives and
two worn-out marriages behind him, and she in her
middle fifties, and yet she could take him by the
heart like that, and he was hers irrecoverably, hers
for ever. Not just until death parted them, either,
but until death put an end to him.

And there in the picture with the Princess von
Werdenberg was her almost equally famous Baron
Ochs von Lerchenau, just blustering out his hopeless
case to the last before her imperious eyes, at once
patrician and boorish, shrewd and gullible, graceless
and yet with a disarming twinkle in his eye. Richard
in well-padded waistcoats – for he had never had
the bulk for Baron Ochs, though he had every other
felicity – carried even his humiliating defeat and the
loss of his Sophie with a flash of style no other bass-
baritone would ever match. Trevor's eyes rested on
him for a long time, and sombrely. Was it possible
to be jealous, painfully, murderously jealous, of an
old man who had never even asserted his pre-
eminence with her in her lifetime, nor exulted in the
proof of it after she was dead?

And where did Dr Randall stand? He was a very
different person from Trevor; he had a wife and a

grown-up family, and his life had been as orderly and consistent as Trevor's had been flamboyant and changeable. And yet if he came in now he would bristle like a terrier raising his hackles at scent of an enemy, and his sharp eyes under their beetling brows would flash from the woman in the magazine to the caressing hand and the veiled glance that lingered upon her, and his mouth would compress its folded lines into obstinate hostility. They were men mad north-north-west only, but Antonia was the magnetic force that disorientated them from their pole. Maybe Trevor was right. There would be no more women like that, never again; the modern world with its monstrous, cumulative complexity could no longer find a place for such prodigies of personality. Look how much room they took up, crowding into the wings all these cramped creatures who should have been people in their own right.

'And she turned her back on the lot of us,' said Trevor, in a light, considering voice, without apparent bitterness. 'All except Richard.'

Richard had paid heavily for that. Susan drank her coffee, and tried to eat, but every morsel stuck in her throat. The whole appalling busines stuck in her throat.

She caught a glimpse of McHugh when she left the dining room. He passed through the hall from the outer door in a gust of frosty air, glowing with vigour and pleasure, and she saw that Trevor had been right. He had already managed to borrow ski trousers and boots from somewhere, and he left dykes of powdery snow outlining his footmarks on the scrubbed boards. The great sweater must have been borrowed, too. He was a man who knew how to acquire what he wanted, wherever he might find himself. She saw him push open the door of the bar and stride in, and presently heard a woman's voice raised between laughter and scolding. That was neither Frau Mehlert nor Liesl; a higher-pitched voice than theirs, with an indefinable impudence about it. McHugh answered in German which was probably execrable and far from extensive, but served his purpose very well, and was used with his invariable brazen confidence.

He came out again as she was passing, and grinned at her amiably, as though they were meeting after a perfectly normal night, untouched by death or crime.

'Hullo, how do you feel this morning? You ought to come out and get some fresh air, do you good. Do you ski? But even if you don't, now's your chance to learn.'

An extraordinary young man, come to think of it, energetic, able, animal; last night, as far as he was concerned, was as dead as Richard.

'I've got no kit,' she said automatically, taking the easiest way of escape.

'Liesl would lend you hers, if you asked her. She's bigger than you, but not so very much, you'd get by in her things. The boots might be a problem, though.'

'Thanks,' said Susan, 'but I won't bother her. I see you managed all right.'

'These?' He laughed, stamping the handsome boots lightly on the scrubbed floor, and smoothing the close black cloth of the trousers. 'I'm lucky. I turned out to be just about the same size as Frau Agathe's husband. And he isn't going to want his things until the road's open again – he's a policeman, stationed

down in Bad Schwandegg, and the big fall caught him
down there, so he can't get home. Seems it happens
to somebody almost every year.'

'You're using his skis, too?' She had always thought
that skis were rather personal things, treasured and
cared for so fastidiously that lending them was rather
like confiding your favourite dog to the care of a
stranger. Evidently Frau Agathe was not afraid to
make free with her husband's possessions. But then,
McHugh was the sort of man who would extract
them from her almost before she knew she was being
manipulated.

The girl came out of the bar with her plastic pail
of hot water, and smiled at them a bright, compre-
hensive smile which nevertheless contrived to
concentrate its brilliance more particularly upon
McHugh. She was very fair and extremely pretty,
with a great plait of yellow hair coiled up on top of
her head. She might have been about twenty-eight
years old, and had the poise of all mountain women,
and a magnificent, erect walk that made her look
taller than in fact she was. Even at walking, thought
Susan, let alone skiing, I couldn't compete.

Frau Agathe pointed to the snowy prints left
melting along the hall, and laughed, and shook an
admonitory finger at the culprit. It was early in the
day to spoil her clean floors, and he could very easily
have stamped off the powdery snow before he came
into the house. He hung his head and made a guilty
face, and then, with the insolence which might have
been expected of him, caught her raised hand by the
wrist, and boxed his own ears with it. The understanding between them was good; the girl opened her
fingers and lent him her palm for the purpose with

perfect complacency. Who but McHugh could do a thing like that and get away with it?

'I'd borrow her things for you,' he said, as Agathe walked smiling away into the kitchen, 'but she'll be wanting them herself when she's finished here. She promised to show me the best slopes. Why don't you ask Liesl?'

'I shouldn't be any good. And I was looking for Neil, actually. I want to talk to him.'

'Oh, well, see you at lunch, then.' And off he went and from the doorway she watched him slide his feet into the grips of the policeman's skis, and clip the springs into the grooves of his boot heels. He launched himself inexpertly but unconcernedly, as though his lack of experience was more than compensated for by his excellent physical co-ordination and boundless self-confidence.

When he was gone she set out purposefully to look for Neil, and found him in the terrace room where Richard's body had been discovered. He had buried himself at a table in the far corner, as though he must have the wall at his back and the whole room spread before him in order to fend off the recollections which pressed in upon him. He had papers spread over the table in front of him, and was poring over them with his face gripped between his hands. She had never seen him look so drawn and grey. McHugh might be immune from doubt or responsibility, but very certainly Neil Everard was not.

She closed the door, and he looked up sharply from his reading. 'Oh, Susan, I was wondering about you.' His eyes went over her in one quick, considerate glance. 'You didn't sleep,' he said with resigned reproach.

'No, I couldn't. I don't think you did much better yourself.' She looked down at the table, and recognised her own handwriting on one of the scattered sheets. 'Have you – seen him this morning? Have they taken him any food?'

He was stung by that, perhaps because of his weariness betrayed into an irritability unusual in him. 'Of course they have,' he said stiffly. 'What do you think I am? Franz took up his breakfast to him. I've been up myself, too, and offered him a bath—'

'Under guard, of course! And he told you to go to hell.'

'He did not. He accepted the chance when it was offered, like a sensible chap.'

Yes, she thought, from you I suppose he might. He's got nothing personal against you.

'Are those the statements we wrote yesterday – this morning? I wanted to ask you about them. I felt we ought to go on considering everything.'

'So did I,' he said, and sighed, averting his eyes. 'Even if there isn't much doubt. There isn't, you know, Susan. No good blinking it.'

'All the same,' she said, 'I'd like to look at them.'

'Of course!' He slid a cushion along the fixed bench by the wall to raise the seat a little for her, and they sat shoulder to shoulder over the sheets of note-paper, tracing the movements of seven people on Christmas Eve.

'No need to tell you about your own movements. Straight from the dining room to the bar after Laurence. You suggested a walk, he went upstairs for his coat, you waited for him below. In the hall you met McHugh coming out from this room – that's about twenty-five past nine to half-past. Laurence came in here and stood talking to Richard for a few moments, then he rejoined you, and the two of you were out until nearly midnight, when you came back and saw Richard still sitting here. Laurence tells much the same story. Naturally he swears he put nothing in Richard's glass, but it's clear he did have the opportunity. Actually in these written statements neither of you went into details about exactly where he stood, how soon Richard looked up, and so on. I suppose it wouldn't occur to you to try to sort out all that until the question was raised.

'Now for me. I went up to my room – in a bit of a huff, I may as well admit – after Mrs Quayne lost her head and went for me. I put away the will safely, and simmered down, and went and had a long, leisurely bath. But it was too early to go to bed. I came down into the bar round about ten, I suppose. The doctor was just going up to bed, we met on the stairs; and according to him he did go to bed, and was there until Laurence woke him just after midnight. I stayed in the bar talking to some of the locals, and had two drinks, and packed up about eleven, when everyone went off to get ready for church.'

'Was McHugh in the bar then?' asked Susan.

'Yes, all the time I was there, and looked as if he had been all the evening. He drinks as well as he does everything else, and it takes as little out of him. He was shooting a very nice line with that pretty girl who helps here – Frau Klostermann.'

'He still is, between ski runs.'

'Then I went to bed, and that's all about me. McHugh himself says he was in the bar all the evening after dinner – with allowance for one trip out to the yard, and one in here with the brandy to Richard. He left the door wide open, as he seems to have found it – it was closed when I came down, by the way, you'll see presently who closed it. As McHugh says, he walked in here with both hands occupied, and it seems pretty certain he really was in the bar all the evening from then on. Not that he could possibly have any motive for wanting Richard out of the way, anyhow.'

Susan read and said nothing, her brows drawn together in an intent frown.

'Three more to go. And they were all in the dining room together, arguing hammer and tongs, until after half-past nine, when you and Laurence went out. Mrs Quayne shot her last bolt about twenty to ten, and flounced out. According to her she went up to bed and stayed there, and her light was out by ten. She says she was asleep when the alarm was given. None of that time can be vouched for absolutely, since she was alone. But so far nobody has mentioned seeing her around, either. She *could* have come down without being seen. She *could* have come into this room to have it out with Richard. She'd made it pretty plain she thought somebody ought to, and as I'd refused— Well, there it is.

'Then Randall. He isn't a man for bars. After Miranda left he says Mason came through and fetched some beer, and they sat and drank it in the dining room. Just before ten he announced his intention of going to bed, and they put out the lights in the dining room and walked through the hall together. Through the door of this room, which was still open, they saw Richard sitting here writing. Randall stopped to call good night to him, Mason went on into the bar. He didn't look back, so he didn't see whether Randall went into the room or not. Randall says he didn't, but he very well could have done. What's evident by his own account is that when he came away he closed the door. As far as we know it remained closed the rest of the evening.'

'Why didn't Laurence?' asked Susan abruptly.

'Mmmm?' He looked up at her, momentarily bewildered.

'Why didn't Laurence close the door? If he'd put morphine in Richard's drink, he wouldn't want him left in full view of anybody who passed, would he? Suppose he fell out of his chair when the coma came on? Suppose someone went by and saw him sprawled on the table? There was every chance of an alarm being given far too soon, and then the doctor would have been called to treat him, and most probably he would have been saved. A murderer would have shut the door to keep him quietly out of sight until it was too late. Why didn't Laurence?'

'Isn't that presupposing that murderers make no mistakes? They probably make more than the rest of us – more than they themselves would in their everyday occupations. You were there waiting for him. Maybe it would have been too pointed to close a door he'd found standing wide open. Maybe he just didn't think of it until later. He wouldn't be at his coolest, would he?'

'No, maybe not. Though it took some nerve, wouldn't you say, to go away and walk about the village with me until midnight, and chance the will being finished and signed before the poison took effect, or somebody finding Richard too soon?'

'Well, he could hardly snatch it away while Richard

was alive, could he? He had to do some gambling, one way or another. And by going out with you he hoped to provide himself with an alibi for the whole time, so that provided the will wasn't signed and valid it wouldn't mattter to him whether it was found or not. He had to take the risk that Richard might live to sign it. But that may well have seemed a lesser risk than staying close to the scene of the crime, or coming back to it too soon.'

'But in that case,' she objected thoughtfully, 'why burn the will at all? If he was so sure of his own alibi, why destroy the will? He had nothing to gain – we know it wasn't signed, because neither McHugh nor anyone else was called to witness it.'

'That doesn't necessarily prove it wasn't signed. If Richard did finish writing, and felt sleep coming on him, how do we know he didn't add his signature, even without witnesses? Maybe Laurence knows enough to know that a court just *might* uphold such a will, if there was sufficiently strong evidence of the genuineness of the signature. In which case it would be crazy to take the risk. Far better to get rid of it.'

There was an answer to everything. The trouble was that she never knew how right the answers were. She frowned down at the doctor's surprisingly precise hand, and said only: 'All right. It was Dr Randall who closed the door, and that was at ten o'clock. Go on, we're down to the last one.'

'Trevor Mason. Trevor's account bears out Randall's to the point where they parted in the hall. After that he says he was in the bar. Certainly he was when I went in there myself, and he stayed there until about twenty past ten, and then said good

night and left. But bear in mind he'd also been
through for the beer at about twenty to ten, and
nobody's mentioned being around at the time to
swear to his movements. He could have looked in
here on his way.

'Now for the Mehlert family. Their accounts are
largely useful as enlarging on the movements of the
rest of us. Mrs Mehlert was in the kitchen baking all
the evening, and saw very little of any of us. Franz
was in the bar most of the time. He served Richard
with two litres of beer in pretty rapid succession, and
remembers his asking for some writing paper, and
carrying off the second litre into this room. Franz
passed through the hall only two or three times
during the evening, but he bears out that this door
stood open at about a quarter to ten, but closed from
about ten.

'It wasn't Franz who served McHugh with the
cognac, that was Frau Agathe. She confirms that he
picked up the two glasses and marched straight
across the hall to bring the one to Richard in here.
One of the foresters, seeing him with both hands full,
opened the door for him. Liesl, who happened to be
coming back after taking a look to see if we'd all quit
the dining room, so that she could clear the table,
saw him put down Richard's drink on the table here,
swap a few words with him, and start back towards
the door. She must have been only a few seconds
ahead of you.'

'She went through into the kitchen just as
Laurence came down the stairs.'

'Then, some time later – he thinks just before half-
past ten – Franz went through the hall for the last
time, and opened this door and looked in to see if

anyone was still here. Richard was still writing, and
told him he'd put out the lights when he finished.
His beer mug was then empty, so Franz brought it
away with him and closed the door again. He says
Richard seemed awake and normal enough then. At
least, he noticed nothing wrong.'

'Did he notice how much of the brandy had been
drunk?'

'That's bright of you,' said Neil approvingly. 'You
remember Randall didn't notice. But Franz was a
practical publican clearing up for the night, and he
wouldn't miss a thing like that. If it had been empty
he'd have brought the glass away, but it wasn't. But
he says the level was down about three-quarters.'

'So we can take it the morphine – papaveretum,
or whatever it is – was in it and taken before that
point.'

'I think we can. No one would dare to doctor it
after it got as low as that. Moreover, it would be
infinitely more difficult as soon as he'd finished his
beer and drew the brandy glass nearer to him. The
doctor wouldn't commit himself on the time when
the dose must have been swallowed. He says the
effect can vary widely with different cases, and
there's no way of knowing how many tablets were
used. But in view of what Franz says we can be
pretty certain the tablets were added between half-
past nine and half-past ten.

'Let's see what we can make of these statements,
then, as regards motive and opportunity. Who had
motive? You, Mrs Quayne, Laurence, Randall, and
Mason all stood to gain substantially if Richard died
intestate. There could be other motives, I suppose,
though I'm damned if I've been able to find any

traces of them up to now. Here was Richard making a will with the expressed intention of squashing any hopes you had in that direction, and before he could finish it he was killed, and the uncompleted will made away with. There was nothing casual about the murder, his wallet's intact, he wasn't robbed.'

'No need to labour it,' said Susan. 'We all know the facts, it's not much good disputing them.'

'So much for motive. Opportunity we must consider in two phases. Opportunity to obtain the morphine, and opportunity to use it. Randall swears his bag was intact just before dinner; he didn't open it then, but he did handle it. And in any case, the only motive we know of didn't appear until the will was read, which was after dinner. Whoever took the morphine took it after that cat was out of the bag. So, then, we have myself: I went upstairs first, while you were all wrangling down here, I had opportunity. So had Miranda, who went up at twenty to ten. So had Laurence, who went up for his coat about half-past nine. So had Trevor, who went to fetch some beer at just after twenty to ten, though he didn't have a lot of time – still, nobody actually timed him. The other three cases are more difficult. You, I suppose, could have rushed upstairs before following Laurence into the bar, no one was watching you; but in view of what follows, thank God, you can rule yourself out. McHugh did have the opportunity to get the morphine while we were all shut in together reading the will, but as he had no motive, didn't know the terms of the will, and wasn't involved in it, I think he can be ruled out, too. Then there's Randall himself. Obviously he could possess himself of tablets from his own bag whenever he liked, but

114

until after dinner I swear he knew nothing about the provisions of the will, so why should he? He didn't know he was going to have a use for it.'

'He wouldn't have had to slit open the bag to get it, either,' said Susan, frowning over the list of names he. had compiled.

'No, but as he pointed out to me, very fairly, that hardly lets him out. If he wanted it for murder he wouldn't simply unlock the bag and take it, would he? That would make him the only possible suspect.'

'No, of course not. And supposing he just happened to have that tube of tablets on him, instead of locked in his bag, when he suddenly acquired an urgent motive for killing Richard? He'd use them, and then slit up the bag afterwards, wouldn't he? To let us all into the picture. And he could have done that at leisure any time after he went to bed at ten.'

'That's true,' said Neil, glumly staring. 'No need to make it even more complicated than it is, but you're right, it could have happened like that. In any case, he can't be ruled out when it comes to having access to the poison. And finally, opportunity to administer the poison. Take the list of those who might have got possession of it. Me – I could have taken it any time I was upstairs, and I could have gone in to Richard and made an opportunity of dropping it into his glass when I came down, I suppose, if I'd had any reason to want to do such a thing. Leave me in. Mrs Quayne was not under anyone's eye from the time she went upstairs, she could have come down again unobserved easily enough. She's in. Laurence – you know about him – he is undoubtedly in. Trevor? Yes, he could have done it, either before he brought back the beer, or

115

when he left the bar at half-past ten, though that's very late. You? No, bless you, you're out. You didn't go near Richard during the whole of the period in question. You say it, Laurence says it, and McHugh says it, and that's enough. McHugh? He's pretty thoroughly covered, too, you can count him out. Randall? Yes, he said good night to Richard at ten, he's in.'

'We're taking a lot for granted, aren't we?' she suggested after some hesitation, 'in supposing that the brandy could have been doctored like that, during an encounter of only a few minutes, and under Richard's very nose? The tablets, even if they're reasonably soluble, wouldn't just vanish in a moment.'

'He wasn't paying any heed to the brandy, he was still drinking his beer. And remember, Richard was busy composing a will, and pretty determined about it, and it would have all his attention. I think any person he knew among us could have leaned over his table, even perched on the edge of it – they're good, solid fixtures – and obscured the glass with his own body while he slipped the tablets into it. And quite simply, it was done. There was no other time when it could have been doctored, it must have been done while it stood on that table. Or have you an alternative suggestion?'

If she had, she kept it to herself, continuing to study the list before her with shadowed eyes. Neil threw down his pen suddenly, and took his face wearily between his hands.

'I don't know what we're hoping to prove,' he groaned. 'We can go on manipulating the times as long as we like, and it won't do away with that bit of burned paper in the safe, or the doctor's phial, either. But I had to go through all the motions, in case something equally suggestive turned up, pointing in the opposite direction. God knows what I was hoping for – I shouldn't like it any better whichever way it pointed. But nothing's turned up, of course, and nothing will. Oh Lord, Susan, I wish it was over! I wish we were safely out of here.'

'It's late to run,' she said, 'it's happened.'

'I wish I knew if it's finished happening, that's all. Once a thing like this begins, who's to know where it's going to stop? Four legatees would get a bigger share each than five, and three a bigger still. It's an invitation to murder, like a tontine.' He pressed his fingertips hard into the dull hollows under his eyes, and shook his head violently. 'Well, we've got him under lock and key, I don't see what more we can do. And I'm damned if I see what else we could have done. A court wouldn't want any more evidence than we've got to bring in a verdict of guilty.'

'No,' agreed Susan, pushing all the scattered papers together into one tidy pile in the middle of the table. She didn't know what she'd been hoping for from them, either, but whatever it was, she hadn't found it. There was no miraculous salvation there.

She got up from the table, and walked restlessly across the room and back, hugging herself as though she felt the cold.

'Neil,' she said abruptly, 'it's not good, I've got to tell you. But you've got to treat what I say as confidential.'

'Of course,' he said blankly, looking up at her in astonishment and concern, 'if you say so.'

'I must have help, and you're the only one I can turn to.' She lifted desperate eyes to his face, and out it came with a rush. 'I was lying when I said I didn't have Laurence under observation all the time he was standing by Richard's table. I saw every move he made. He couldn't possibly have dropped anything in the glass without my knowing. He couldn't, and he didn't. Neil, he's absolutely innocent.'

CHAPTER IX

They all have double faces! All of them
together!

Act 3

Neil sat gripping the table, staring at her with great
bruised eyes of doubt and consternation. *'What?'* he
said in an almost voiceless whisper. 'But *why*? Why
did you tell such a lie? If you could have cleared him
at once, why on earth didn't you?'

'Because I saw a chance of finding out who *had*
done it. Because when that purely accidental set of
his prints turned up on the glass, and McHugh
jumped like a tiger to seize on them as proof of guilt
– which was damned silly, if we hadn't all been so
on edge – I suddenly realized that the real murderer
would be looking for a scapegoat, and by sheer
incredible luck had picked on the one person who
could be *proved* innocent. Laurence was with me all
the evening, and I *knew*, I could testify absolutely
that he never put a hand near that glass.

'Then I don't see why you didn't say so.' His temper
was rising now, and no wonder, when she remembered to what cumulative horrors her impulse had led
them all, and what compunction Neil must be feeling
for his part in Laurence's horrible night. 'Honestly,
Susan, this is a fine thing to throw at us now—'

'I know it is, I'm not ducking, I'm trying to tell you why, if you'll listen. What would have happened if I'd cleared him on the spot? The murderer would only have waited for the next lead and acted on that, and his second choice mightn't have had a witness to swear to his movements. Look at that list! Mightn't have had? He *wouldn't* have had! Only Laurence and I spent the whole evening together. Someone else would have been dragged into the mud, and we still shouldn't have known who was behind it.'

'And what, for God's sake,' he demanded hotly, 'did you hope to achieve by throwing fuel on the fire? You didn't just refrain from clearing him, you threw in additional evidence. It was you who told us he'd gone upstairs to fetch his coat. It was you who pointed out he'd had the chance to steal the morphine, as well as to use it.'

'I know I did. I wanted to encourage the murderer to think he was on the right horse, and could safely go ahead. I wanted him to take the hint, and plant the clinching evidence on Laurence. I was fore-warned, I meant to make sure he was caught doing it. He couldn't have planted it already, you see. How could he? How did he know which way the evidence was going to point? He had to wait and see which of us fate elected to be chief suspect, and *then* help the good work along. So all I had to do was confirm him in his choice of Laurence, and then make sure nobody got to Laurence's room before I did. He couldn't plant evidence actually on him, not while we were all in the same room together. No, it had to be his room, and it had to be done quickly. And even if my gamble didn't come off, you see, and nothing was planted after all, I could get Laurence

120

out of his mess at any time by telling the truth. I didn't think there was any risk of anything worse than a bad hour or so for him, and maybe one almost as nasty for me.'

'But, Susan, this is fantastic—'

'So's murder, isn't it? Maybe it looks fantastic to you now, but it made sense then to me. As soon as there was mention of searching I knew we should have to split up, and the only other woman was his mother. I could manage her if I had to. As it turned out I didn't have to, she disposed of herself very effectively, and when you sent me upstairs with Liesl I was dead sure everything was going to work out.'

Neil's drawn brows, levelled into a single long line, scowled at her. 'You mean you repeated all this farrago to Liesl? She was supposed to exercise supervision over you, not to do what *you* told *her*.'

'I did tell her what to do. I didn't have time to tell her why, but I must have been convincing, because she didn't argue. We rushed to my room, and I changed quickly, and she had a look through my things, and then we went to Laurence's room. The door wasn't locked, and we left it ajar so that we could hear when anyone came up the stairs. We weren't going to be making any noise ourselves, so it wouldn't be difficult to hear. We hid there and waited. I thought he was sure to come, because he *had* to. If I could make a way of getting there, so could he. We were behind the window curtains, we should have been able to see everything. Only he didn't come. It all went horribly wrong. When we did at last hear someone coming it was the whole lot of you crowding up the stairs, and we had to scramble out and rush to meet you, so that you wouldn't find us in the wrong corridor.'

'Well, go on!' said Neil grimly. 'Finish the tale, now you've taken it so far. No one came in and hid anything, and yet when we searched that room we found the phial, damned well hidden, and the remains of the will, hurriedly but almost completely burned.'

'I know we did. But not by him! When could he have done it, tell me that!'

'The phial was no problem. He hid that as soon as he'd taken the tablets from it, before he came down to join you for your walk. And when you came back at midnight he let you go upstairs ahead of him, and then rushed in here to fetch the will. It wouldn't take him long to burn the thing in his own room before going to wake the doctor. It was done in a hurry, or he'd have made a more thorough job of it. Now you tell me when anyone else but Laurence could have planted them. Go ahead and tell me!'

'I can't,' she owned, halting before him. 'Somehow he – the murderer, whoever he is – must have made sure of his choice earlier. I don't know how, I don't know why, but he must have chosen Laurence, and planted his evidence accordingly. There's a great deal I don't know, but I do know this, Laurence didn't poison Richard Hellier. I *know* it. I never took my eyes from him, and I *know*. So we've got to try other ways of getting at the murderer, quickly, for everyone's sake.' She leaned forward over the table, and gripped his hands convulsively in hers. 'Neil, help me! You must help me!'

The uncontrolled desperation of the gesture, coming from her, had shaken him like a shock of sudden cold. His hands quivered under hers, and then opened and took them in gently. 'I don't understand what you want me to do,' he said in a softer voice, but with some constraint. 'We did everything we could think of doing at once, and you know what we found. If you have reason to suspect someone else you must in justice speak out. For you do see, don't you, that you haven't shown me any such reason yet.'

'I can only tell you those things that have had their effect on me. Whether you'll call them reasons is another matter. You see, I started with the know-ledge that it wasn't Laurence. That gave me an advantage while all the rest of you were watching him. But think, Neil!' She was trembling with eagerness, and felt that the circumstance only made her less convincing, but she could not control it. 'Who was it who jumped in and began to make himself so useful, testing for fingerprints? The one man who'd made sure that his had a perfect right to be there, and wouldn't be questioned, the man who bought the drinks. Who jumped to call attention to those accidental prints of Laurence's as though they were proof positive of guilt, when obviously, if we'd had time to think, they were nothing of the kind? Who found the burned will when Franz failed to question it? Who openly reminded us that he wasn't one of us lucky legatees, and hadn't any connection in the world with Mrs Byrne or Richard, beyond a temporary business engagement? McHugh! Always McHugh!'

'But, girl, you're crazy!' said Neil, kindly but very firmly. 'You yourself said it, he has nothing to do with it. What if he does shout about having no motive? It doesn't alter the fact he really has none.

He's only here at all because he happened to be detailed to the job of flying us over by his bosses at European Charter.'

'How do we know that? What do we know about him – him, the person, not the pilot? He was the one who rushed to elect somebody else as the criminal, on the flimsiest grounds then, you must admit it. He's the one about whom none of us knows anything, he's the one nobody's watching.'

'Except you,' said Neil, with the tired ghost of a smile.

She was not sure that she liked that smile, or the resigned tone of his voice, the note of reserve in its disinterested kindness. 'There could be no harm in looking into his background a little, could there?'

'I suppose not, but how can we? We haven't even a telephone connection with the outside world, you know that. If I could call European Charter in London I would, but I can't. So what do you want me to do?'

She saw then how it was with him, and in her heart she couldn't blame him. He had been thrust into accidental responsibility for all of them, and he'd carried it well, but it had given him a very nasty time, and he shrank, mind and spirit, from reopening what now seemed a closed case. Even the police must feel like that on occasion. Probably they do drag themselves out of harbour again and venture back reluctantly into the offshore currents if there seems a grain of doubt left; but then, Neil wasn't a policeman, and he was offered, in the end, an easier kind of salvation. Two more days of this weather and the track to Bad Schwandegg would be open, and the proper authorities would be able to take the whole

burden from him. No, she couldn't blame him for
being loath to put to sea again with retirement so
near. All the same, she did her best.

'You could finish what we didn't finish last night,'
she said urgently. 'Don't free Laurence yet, don't tell
them what I've told you, let the murderer go on
thinking he's safe. Only you'll tell Laurence, won't
you, and put his mind at rest? Tell him I'm not as
bad as he thinks me – he'll never listen to me. And
you and Franz go quietly and search everyone else's
belongings as thoroughly as you did his—'

'What, without letting them be present? Without
saying a word to them? What a scandalous thing to
suggest!'

'Why? You said you were going to do it last night.
If Franz does the searching I don't see how they can
complain. It was only by accident, because he made
that childish challenge of his, that we began with
Laurence, but after the things we found there we
never looked any farther. We ought to have done.
We ought to have gone through everybody's things.
The police would have done.'

'But we'd found what we were looking for.'

'I know. I'm not blaming you, it was an obvious
mistake to make, we were all at fault. If we'd gone
on there might have been other highly significant
things to be found, even though we didn't know
enough to be consciously looking for them. We
shouldn't simply have assumed that we'd finished
when the phial of tablets turned up. The police
wouldn't have let it go at that.'

She was not even sure that she was telling the strict
truth now, but with a correct legal conscience like
his he ought to find that argument impressive. He

did seem to be wavering, though she could see him shrinking perceptibly from the necessity for pricking the entire party back into desperate enmity. Then as visibly he stiffened against her.

'I think, Susan, you're forgetting the nature of the finds we did make. They're as nearly conclusive as anything could be, and you've pointed out yourself, more clearly than ever, that they couldn't have been planted at any time after the alarm was given. I don't believe any police force in the world would hesitate to charge him on that evidence.'

'What, *now*? When I've *proved* him innocent? I've told you, Laurence *did not do it*! He didn't, he couldn't, I never took my eyes from him while he was in this room with Richard. That isn't hearsay, there's no maybe about it, it's absolute fact. So the rest of the evidence against him must be so many lies, it can't be anything else. It's evidence in reverse, evidence against someone else, if we have the sense to make use of it, and try to understand what it has to tell us.' She was shouting at him now in her desperation, shaking his hands vehemently in hers.

He disengaged himself gently, drawing back from her. The troubled mask of doubt and reserve had come down over his face and shut him out of reach. She had been too insistent, not nearly clever enough. If she had laid the load of choice on him squarely, and had the restraint to leave him to resolve it for himself he would surely have driven himself into action. Now she had said too much too fiercely. He was looking at a woman in a purposeful rage, not after justice, but after some female interest of her own; and it was too late to tread gently now and try to undo what she had done.

'Laurence isn't charged yet,' he said with careful calm. 'He's not in custody. He's perfectly safe where he is, and nothing can possibly be done in the matter, one way or the other, until the police get here. A matter of two days, three at the most, if this weather holds.'

'In two days,' she said, 'vital evidence that we might have found last night will have been disposed of.'

'It's too late to worry about that, I'm afraid. Already several hours have passed since we stopped our search, that's time enough for things to have been disposed of already. You may very well be right in saying we ought to have gone ahead then, and I wish to God we had, but we didn't. What's the point of resuming now? No, I see nothing further we can usefully do. In a few days we shall hand over everything to the police, and you will of course tell them exactly what you've just told me. Then it will be up to them. You can be sure Laurence will get the benefit of any doubt there may be.'

'*Doubt?*' For a moment she could hardly believe she had heard him correctly. She put up her hands dazedly and felt at her temples, staring at him between her compressing fingers in fascination and terror. 'I'm telling you there isn't any doubt. Can't you understand? I'm not saying he may not have done it, I'm telling you he *didn't* do it. Doubt is what doesn't exist. This is certainty.'

He looked back at her unhappily, and said only: 'You must tell that to the police. It will be up to them, of course, whether they believe you.'

'*Believe* me?' she whispered. 'You mean *you don't?*'

'I don't say that! But, Susan, for God's sake try to

127

see it from my point of view. You did say the flat opposite at first, you know. Here's the same person telling two opposing stories on two consecutive days, one of them has to be a lie. When somebody who's lied once picks out one of the stories and says: "This is the true one," how do we know whether it is or not? How can we tell. *You* say you lied yesterday for a good reason, to try to trap the real murderer, but somebody else might wonder if you weren't telling the truth yesterday, when this was sprung on you without warning, and lying today, when you've had a night to think things over. You – well, you're – interested in Laurence, aren't you? At least, I did think there were signs of it. You're sorry for him, maybe you're even persuading your own memory to hedge about details because you feel it was you who got him into this. I – forgive me, I'm not saying this is what I think, I'm trying to show you what could be argued. People might reason that you'd been considering that you and Laurence both stood to inherit about sixty thousand pounds of Mrs Byrne's money – more, if one of the others is convicted of Richard's murder—'

Susan closed her eyes, for the room was revolving slowly and drunkenly about her. She had never fainted in her life, but then, she had never before been suspected of being an accessory after the fact in a murder case, on top of a sleepless night and an agonised examination of her own disastrous actions. She was aware of arms snatching her up as she fell, and stiffened at the touch, her rebellious senses springing back into quivering life. She opened her eyes again to see Dr Randall's face bending over her.

Someone had lifted her into a chair; that must have

been Neil. But it was the doctor's hand that was holding a glass to her lips. He had made a very apt entrance, and a very quiet one, unless her ears had ceased to function for longer than she had supposed. How much had he heard of those last exchanges? People who walk as softly as that, even on bare wooden floors, sometimes arrive at doors quite unheard, and may well be sufficiently interested in the conversation within to linger for a few minutes before silencing it with the full stop of the door opening. You never can tell, when there's a murderer in the house.

'Your turn this time,' Dr Randall was saying resignedly. 'As if I haven't got enough on my hands with the one upstairs. Go on, girl, drink it, it isn't poisoned. I always have a day off on Christmas Day.'

Wouldn't you know, thought Susan, shivering at the bitter astringent taste on her tongue, that when life finally exasperated Dr Randall into making a joke it would be that kind of joke? She drank, and pushed the hand away from her. Neil's arm was round her shoulders, and his face, hovering over her doubtfully, was concerned and kind and deeply troubled. She felt almost as sorry for him as for herself.

'I'm all right,' she said resolutely.

'You can't miss your night's sleep and take it in your stride, you young people. It's only the old who're tough enough to stand up to this kind of thing. What's Everard been doing to you? No, sit still! I don't doubt you're all right, but don't be in too big a hurry to prove it, you've got all day.' He put down the glass, and stood frowning down at her from under his bushy brows. 'You'd be well advised to go out and get a breath of air, while the sun's out, if you feel up to it. You're going to see more than enough of the inside of this house before today's over.'

It seemed to her a good idea. She had to get away from them all, and think what was to be done next, since Neil wasn't to be budged from his position, and had enlightened her only too successfully about the untenable nature of hers. She got to her feet experimentally, and her legs bore her up steadily; the lapse was over.

'Thanks, I think I will. I'm quite all right now, it was nothing.'

At the door, feeling their eyes following her, she turned. Both the watching faces were wary and intent; their constraint was for each other as well as for her.

'You'll bear in mind what I've said, won't you, Neil?'

'Yes, I promise you I will. I shouldn't discuss it with anyone else, if I were you,' said Neil in a carefully casual voice. 'Anyone outside, I mean.'

'No, naturally I won't.' She went out and closed the door, her heart beating a little more hopefully. Even if he wouldn't take action, maybe he was still thinking it over, maybe he'd come round to believing her in the end. Why should he agree to become even so far her confederate unless he was making some reassessments in his own mind?

When she let herself out by the front door she stepped into flooding sunshine, and her heart lurched upward into her throat. Under the lee of the terrace room, beneath the glass wall, McHugh was reclining on his skis, basking with closed eyes and a contented smile, and occasionally whistling very softly to prove that he was not asleep. Two days of this, and he would have acquired that peculiar golden-yellow tan mountain sunshine and snow provide between them; he was sure to tan with the same combination of efficiency and luck with which he did everything else. Above his head the façade of glass rose, perforated at the top by the grid of an extractor fan. She wondered, even before he opened one eye and trained it smilingly upon her, how long he had been there; she was mortally afraid that it was too long. Neil had been late in warning her; they should have looked out of the window before they raised their voices.

CHAPTER X

'Tis sport for brazen rogues like you.

Act 1

Neil couldn't be blamed, she had brought it on herself. Or rather, and that was the most terrible thing about it, she had brought it not on herself but on Laurence. But how could she have dreamed that when she did tell the truth she wouldn't be believed, she who had never before in her life told a really successful lie? How could she ever have supposed that the lifeline she had held in reserve with such absolute confidence would break and let Laurence fall to his death? She had created this awful situation, it was more than ever up to her to resolve it successfully. If Neil would not help her she must go ahead alone. There were two things, at least, she could try to do; get a message to Laurence, not to justify herself but to do what could be done to reassure him; and search McHugh's belongings, the only present means she had of investigating the man himself.

She sought out Liesl after lunch, and spent some time working up to the suggestion that Liesl should make use of the house keys to let her into Laurence's room; and when that was gently but firmly refused, that Liesl should carry Laurence a note when she took in his dinner tray. But it seemed that Franz was taking care of the prisoner's needs in person, and had forbidden his daughter to enter the room; a natural enough view for a father to take of murderers, when she came to think of it, and what else could Laurence be to him? After that she let the Mehlerts alone, and tried slipping a note under the locked door in a quiet moment around the tea hour, when everyone else was downstairs, but she got no acknowledgement for it, and knew in her heart that he would toss it into the wastebasket as soon as he saw her handwriting. Before she went downstairs again she tried McHugh's door. His room was next to hers on the balcony that clung to the front of the house, and like hers had a long window on this wooden platform under the wide eaves, but both door and window were secured. The door looked very like her own; if the locks matched, a little private practice in her own room might enable her to break into his. But not yet, not while the house was wide awake and populous.

Miranda did not appear all day, which at an ordinary time Susan would have esteemed as a merciful dispensation; but now her absence weighed even more heavily than her presence would have done. Dr Randall reported her as calmer, and not really ill, but Laurence wasn't his son, and maybe he was taking altogether too detached a view.

McHugh came indoors when the afternoon sun thinned and grew pale. Susan saw him cruise down vigorously from the meadows, laughing at his own shaken security when he ran from the untrodden planes on to the beaten and frozen snow of the roadway. Frau Agathe was beside him, keeping his speed with ease, checking and turning to correct his errors, and guiding him with advice and encouragement like a young mother helping her baby with his first steps. In dark-brown ski trousers and a thick corn-yellow sweater, with a woollen cap pulled down over her fair hair, she looked like the most leisured and lovely of the winter tourists who never found their way up here to Obershwandegg. She brought him safely to the doorway, slapped from his seat the snow of his last fall, and flashed away homewards still laughing; and presently, having lodged his skis in the rack in the porch, he came in glowing and crashed up the stairs to change, whistling softly to himself and looking sleek and fed like a cat full of cream.

An hour later Frau Agathe came in to begin her evening's work, sedate and feminine and clearly of local growth in her loden cloak and full skirts. Susan sat in the corner of the bar, after dinner, and watched McHugh's indoor technique, which was as impressive as his outdoor one. He had reached the point at which he could stroll behind the bar and lift down bottles for himself without being obtrusive about it. Had he advanced so far last night? No one had mentioned it, but his gift was for doing that kind of thing without exciting comment. Was he on the near side of the bar or behind it when Agathe poured out the cognac? And how much would Agathe do for him? Take his word for something and pledge it as her own? Lie for him? Or even— No, beyond that nothing. She was lighthearted and gay, and liked being liked, and she was as ready for a diversion as he was, but there was nothing about her dishonest or corruptible. But there are more ways than one of making use of a woman.

The brandy must have been poisoned as it stood at Richard's elbow, Neil had said: there was no other possibility. But Neil could be wrong, must be wrong. She was sure of her man. Why should McHugh have dropped the first tentative, flimsy seed of suspicion against Laurence, unless he was covering up for himself? And how could he have pounced unerringly upon the twist of blackened paper in the ashtray, if he had not known where to look for it, and exactly what he would find written on it? No, she could not be wrong. Even his extraordinary and misdirected energy could hardly account for that brief and mischievous career of his as a detective. He knew where to find the burned will because it was he who had burned it and left it there to be found. Only when Franz had passed it by with no more than a glance had McHugh taken charge. If you want a thing done well, do it yourself.

'At least one person seems to be enjoying himself in Oberschwandegg,' said Trevor, coming to her side with a glass of white vermouth in his hand. 'One wonders if Herr Klostermann has disturbed dreams, down there in the valley.'

'He might have those, in the circumstances,' said Susan, 'even if there was no such person as McHugh. She's a very attractive girl.'

'She is. He's probably spending the nights praying for fair weather, and the days digging. Odd he should be a policeman,' he said with a grimace. 'There'll be a welcome for him when he does get through, if not from his wife. He can't get here too soon for me.'

Susan had no wish for company, and no energy to spare from watching McHugh. She was wondering for how long he might be regarded as immobilised here, and how soon the corridors upstairs would be deserted enough for her to risk an attempt on his door. She was, in fact, reaching the moment when she felt encouraged to say good night and withdraw, when McHugh rose in his place, stretching and hiding a yawn, and took the words clean out of her mouth.

'Lord, I'm sleepy! I haven't had so much fresh air for years. I'm going to have an early night.' He said his good night across the room to them in English, and to the room in general in German, patted Frau Agathe quite respectfully on the shoulder, and went placidly out of the room.

'He's right, you know,' said Susan, taking the cue, though with disappointment and dismay for a chance thrown away. Not ten o'clock yet, and she had been relying on him to be the last to retire, not the first! But at least if he was really going to bed she could go, too; not to sleep, maybe, but at least to be quiet and alone. She had had more than enough of this day. 'We none of us got much rest last night,' she said. 'I think I'll go, too. Good night, Trevor.'

'One day nearer home tomorrow,' said Trevor, smiling at her.

That was one way of looking at it, and he meant it kindly. But how did it look to Laurence in his remote room at the end of the wing? She had been thinking of him every moment of the day, far more clearly and accurately than if he had been present by her side; it was as if in his absence she had spent an age getting to know him.

She let herself into her own room, and sat on the bed listening to the brisk sounds from next door. There was this to be said for McHugh, he made no secret of his presence; wherever it might happen to suit him to be, he was always clearly audible. His progress towards bed was marked by a succession of loud and unmistakable sounds, the crash of one shoe falling, then the other, the energetic thudding of his bare feet about the floor, the loud flow of his tap and the gurgle of a vociferous waste pipe. He sang his way to the bathroom and whistled his way back. She could not exactly hear the snap of the switch when he turned off his light, but the abrupt cessation of sound that followed was so noticeable as to be almost a sound in itself. One would have thought his every move was calculated to inform his neighbours.

It was some time before it dawned upon her that this stray thought might be very close to the truth. Her own light was out, and she was lying fully dressed on her bed, wondering wretchedly whether it was any use making one more attempt to get Laurence to listen to her. Miserably rehearsing gambits which should induce him not to shut his ears, she heard the soft creak of springs from the bed in the next room, and sat up in the dark, holding her breath.

A very different sound, this, from those which had marked his retirement. If she had not been wide awake and straining her ears in the silence she would not have caught it. She leaned her head against the wall between them, and traced with quivering attention the stealthy rustling of clothes, the soft padding of feet as he stepped off the rugs on to the boards, hardly sounds at all, mere stirrings in the silence. No doubt of it, McHugh was out of bed again, and dressing.

The luminous hands of her watch showed just after midnight. While he was still making small movements of his own which might cover hers, she tiptoed to the door and eased back the latch, leaving the door ajar, so that when he left his room she might look out without any betraying noise. Whatever he was up to about the house at this time, after his elaborately public retirement at ten o'clock, she must observe it. She sat waiting for the click of his door opening; but what she heard was the sound of a bolt sliding back in its socket, and it came from the wrong side of the room. He was opening the long window on to the balcony.

She parted the curtains and peered along towards his room, and in a moment heard the slow, faint creak of the hinges as the window was opened. At the end of the house front a wooden staircase led down to the ground; the snow had been shovelled from the steps, there would be no trace of his passing except, perhaps, the darkening of the film of frost which lay over the cleared treads.

She saw a long arm flattened against the glass, and then he stepped out into the starry night, and very quietly, very gently, closed the window after him. The latch settled into place soundlessly. With long, light steps he slipped along the balcony and began to descend the staircase. She saw the bulky darkness of a duffle coat, and a glimpse of his face as he cast one quick glance behind.

Hurriedly she dragged on her coat, and tugged at the bolts of her own window. He must be on the ground by now, and even if he looked back again she would not be visible until she left the shadow of the eaves and ventured down the steps after him. She hugged the wall of the house, where the darkness clung, and from behind the carved corner post at the top of the steps she saw him against the snow, striding away along the village street in the direction of the church. There was no moon, but the faint starlight showed up clearly any movement against the pervading whiteness. He was a confident creature, he would not look back now that he was clear of the house. But she would have to keep a good distance between them, and pass quickly from doorway to doorway and gate to gate, in case he did turn his head.

She was so absorbed now in action that she was not consciously thinking at all. All her energy went into the intensity with which she watched him, and the concentration with which she stole down the staircase after him, and crept along the cleared track between the crouching, broad-roofed houses. From head to foot he was mystery; he scarcely had an identity at all, he was merely the pilot who had brought them here. Sooner or later he must make some unwary motion which would shed a more exact light upon himself; or a more definitive darkness.

He had left the road; one instant she saw him, the next he was gone. She hurried, in a panic that she might lose him altogether, but he had only turned into a narrow alley between the houses, where the deep snow was tramped into treacherous ice, and she had to cling to the stakes of the fences on either side to keep herself upright. He plunged straight ahead, relying on his immaculate balance and letting his feet slide like skis. The shadows of the houses covered her gratefully here. And now he was still; he had stopped with his shoulder braced against a narrow door in the high fence. Susan heard the latch lift with a rustle of frosty metal, and he was inside the small yard of a house, and feeling his way cautiously round towards a shuttered window. She watched him through the pales of the fence. He was merely a darkness in motion in the midst of a still darkness, but by the small bars of light that fell through the heart shapes cut in the shutters she caught one brilliant glimpse of his profile, smiling, pleased, complacent. In her heart she knew everything then, but her mind was set on another ending, and she was unwilling to know.

She was quite close to him, braced stiffly against one of the thicker posts of the fence. She heard him rap at the shutters very softly; there was no need for more. A door was opened in the dark bulk of the house; only a faint light came from within, but Susan was accustomed to the darkness now, and it was enough. Before the paler space was filled with McHugh's dark bulk she saw clearly the round white arm reach up to encircle his neck, and the flood of fair hair that flowed over his sleeve. For one instant she looked full into Frau Agathe's face over his shoulder, and saw delight and despair and terror and helpless longing all wildly mingled in the great excited eyes and eager, apprehensive mouth. Then he swept her inside in his arms, and the door closed upon them softly, and the house was quiet; and after a while the light behind the shutters went out.

Susan remained standing by the fence for some minutes more, for want of the will and the purpose to move. She felt a little sick, not because of her own involuntary part as the spy at this meeting, but because of her stupidity in not guessing from the first where he was bound. She should have known enough about him by now, on his own showing, to know that he played his games to a finish; nothing less would ever satisfy him. But the poor fool of a girl! What had she done to herself and that wretched young policeman of hers, chafing helplesly down there in Bad Schwandegg? She wasn't of the stuff McHugh should have encountered, she hadn't his self-absorption or his ruthlessness; or – and that had suddenly become clear as glass in one twilit glimpse of her – his experience. Her gallantries had stopped short of this until now. She was no match for her partner, and he could not give her his own amoral tranquillity of mind, for which yesterday did not exist. My God, thought Susan, shivering in the dark, Oberschwandegg has good reason to curse the wind that blew us here for Christmas.

But there they were, and they could not get away, there was nothing to be done about it. It dawned upon her in a moment or two that Frau Agathe's disaster was her opportunity. McHugh had left himself a way of getting back into his room when he returned. There was no need to consider picking locks now. Nor was she likely to be interrupted for a long time to come, more than long enough for her purpose.

She hurried back to the Horse in the Meadows and let herself into McHugh's room. He had left the curtains drawn over the window, and slipped out between them, and they were heavy and thick enough to screen the bedside lamp; there was no need for her to grope in the dark. She put on the light and looked round a room very like her own, with the same pale wooden furniture, the same massive bed and rugs of brightly coloured wool. In the open bed the hollow left by McHugh's big young body preserved in its clear outline something of his challenging assurance and brazen lightness of heart. Anticipation hadn't made him restless, he must have lain as relaxed as a cat. After all, it was almost a concession on his part to make a pretence of decency and enjoy his triumph in secret. It had taken him just two days to achieve what she was sure nobody had ever accomplished before; by his standards he probably should have been crowing from the rooftop.

She had remembered in time to take off her boots, before the warmth of the room thawed the rims of frost from round the soles and heels, and left wet stains on the pale wood of the floor. She put them outside on the balcony, and drew the window closed again. There was no hurry. She could afford to be methodical, and make sure that she left everything exactly as she found it.

She worked her way steadily through the clothes in his wardrobe, emptying every pocket. Then the few things folded away on the shelves, and the contents of his leather toilet case. He was not a man who burdened himself with very many possessions, apparently, but his clothes were good, casual but well made. There were no books; evidently he did not read. She found two magazines, both from England, one a motoring journal, the other consisting exclusively of variations on the theme of the female, and meant exclusively for the male.

Some of his clothes were very delicately and expertly mended. What did that indicate, a doting mother or a devoted wife? It had never occurred to her that he might be a married man, and even now she did not take the idea seriously until she opened

143

the letter case that lay in the drawer of his bedside table, and found herself looking at a photograph of McHugh domesticated. It was framed behind a thin sheet of celluloid in the front of the case, and it showed him sitting on a lawn playing with a baby boy about a year old, while a young woman sat beside them in a deck chair and beamed impartially upon them both. It could have been his married sister and her baby, of course, or even the wife of a friend of his, but somehow they had the unmistakable look of a married couple, and happily married at that. It was a novel thought that McHugh was probably, in his own fashion, an excellent, considerate, and satisfying husband. And yet – two days this particular conquest had taken him, and was even that his record?

It went against the grain with her to touch his letters, but she set her jaw and examined at least the opening of every one, and as soon as it became clear that they were personal and innocuous put them thankfully back into their envelopes. If Laurence had not been so eternally present in her mind she would have given up in disgust, but what right had she to any scruples? But the little bundle of correspondence thinned down to the last postcard, and showed her nothing but an ordinary young man, complete with family and friends, employer and colleagues.

In his briefcase there was more interesting material, but of a kind which did not help her. Here in another leather folder he kept the nondomestic part of his life. There were photographs of eight girls in all, dark and fair, sleek and sporting, he had no special prejudices. Many of the pictures bore affectionate inscriptions and dates, and the range

was as wide as Europe, with one charming little
Malay Chinese as an exotic touch. Susan wondered
if he had yet asked Frau Agathe for a picture for his
gallery, or whether, indeed, he ever had to ask.

By the time she had finished she was in tears,
though she could not have explained why. There was
such a sadness about this pilgrimage of pleasure that
she would have given anything to have been able to
wash away the knowledge of it, and see Agathe's
tragi-comedy as at least unique, instead of merely
one in a chain of exactly similar incidents. She put
everything carefully back in its place, and stood up
from the rug a little stiffly, rubbing impatiently at
her eyes with the back of her hand. That was that,
and she could hardly say she was no wiser, but
certainly she was no nearer discovering any
connection between McHugh and Richard Hellier, or
any motive McHugh might have for wanting Richard
out of the way.

She put out the light and let herself cautiously out
of the room again, slipping her feet into her boots
on the frosty balcony. Under the stars the village lay
asleep, and it was nearly half-past one in the
morning. She closed McHugh's window and stole
quietly into her own room. The feeling of guilt and
shame eased from her mind gradually; she had taken
nothing, and she would never tell anything, it was
as though she had never invaded his privacy. All the
same, she had achieved nothing, and Laurence was
still a prisoner.

She might as well try her luck with him once more,
since she was wide awake, and the house was fast
asleep. She took off her boots and went in stockinged
feet along the main corridor and round the corner

to the narrow passage on which only one door opened. She stood with her cheek pressed to the panels, listening, but the silence was absolute. He must be asleep. It seemed almost a cruelty to try and wake him, but she rapped softly with her knuckles, and then more sharply with her nails; and then she was caught into the panicky desire to hear his voice, to know that he was there, even if he spoke only to tell her again to go to hell.

There are silences and silences. Some seem to hear and reject you, some are populated and warm but refuse speech, some are remote and impervious, deaf, dumb, and blind. The silence within Laurence's room hung motionless and dead, not vindictive against her, only unaware of her.

'Laurence, are you awake? Laurence, listen to me! Say something! Laurence, wake up!'

Her voice had sharpened until it seemed to her frighteningly loud, and the little blows of her nails on the wood rang like hammers, but nothing answered and nothing moved. Not even the rustling and stirring of an uneasy body in the bed, not even a disturbed breath as her voice penetrated but could not break his sleep. Nothing.

CHAPTER XI

Help, help! A surgeon! Murder, murder, murder!

Act 2

Liesl sat up in bed with a squeak of fright at the first touch of a hand on her cheek, and caught up the bedclothes to her breast. Susan took her by the shoulders and held her still, and the draught from the door she had left open in her haste folded them both in a curl of colder air.

'Ssssh, it's only me, Susan Conroy. Liesl, I want the key of Laurence's room. I've got to have it, quickly. Where is it?'

'In the kitchen,' said Liesl, astonished into making a direct answer, and shrank and hardened into wakefulness at the sound of her own startled voice. 'But you can't have it. You know I mustn't. My father—'

'I know, but this is urgent. There's something wrong in there. I can't get a sound out of him. I've got to get in.'

'But you know he is behaving so,' said Liesl, gaining confidence rapidly. 'He does not wish to speak to you, that is all it is.'

'I tell you it isn't. He'd have spoken by now, all right, if he was able. He'd have told me to get to hell and leave him alone. We've got to go and see. Get the key!'

'I cannot,' said Liesl firmly. 'I am not allowed. And why are you still dressed, in the middle of the night? I think I should tell my father all of this.'

'Tell him what you like, tell whoever you like, I don't care, but get me the key first.' Susan took firm hold of the billowing white feather quilt, and hauled it from the bed. 'Come on, get up! If you don't I'll go and look for it myself. And if he's ill or dying in there, remember to tell everyone you wouldn't help him, won't you?' She caught up the thick woollen dressing gown that lay over the back of the nearest chair, and bundled it into Liesl's reluctant arms. 'Hurry! I tell you I'm scared, there's something terribly wrong.'

'There cannot be,' said Liesl crossly, but struggling into the sleeves in some haste, nonetheless. 'He was quite well when my father saw him at eleven o'clock. The doctor said he had taken cold, so I spiced some wine for him, and my father took it up to him.'

'Maybe it's more than a cold. Maybe he's been taken ill. Come with me and let's take a look at him, at least. He can't get away – how can he? There's nowhere to run to, even if he wanted to run. And there are two of us.' She was wringing her hands with impatience as she hustled Liesl towards the door. The words were only stimulants now, to snap at Liesl's heels like Corgis after cattle, and make her hurry. 'Run – *please*! I'll wait for you by his door.'

Liesl fluttered down the stairs silently in her felt slippers, and silently came again with the big, old-fashioned key. The rear rooms had never been thoroughly modernised, and the lock of Laurence's

door was large enough and ponderous enough for a
prison, and sunk completely into the wood. Almost
before Liesl could turn the key and lift the latch
Susan was thrusting impatiently past her towards the
bed, and reaching for the switch of the bedside lamp.

Neither the sound of the door opening nor the
agitated rush of their entry disturbed Laurence; even
when the cone of light sprang up and flooded his face
he made no move. He lay on his back, his head
turned a little towards them, drawing great, slow,
shallow breaths. His face was livid, the cheeks fallen
into bluish hollows, shadowy stains round his parted
lips. The pale domes of his closed eyelids stood out
in exaggerated relief from the gaunt, bruised hollows
of their sockets. He looked as Richard had looked,
dead, but because of his youth infinitely more
pathetic and helpless. But he was breathing.

Susan fell on her knees by the bed, took his face
between her hands, shook his head gently in her
palms, chafed his cheeks. He submitted to every
impertinence without a sign of awareness. She
turned her chin upon her shoulder to hiss at Liesl,
who was staring in fascinated horror: 'Fetch the
doctor! Quickly! Tell him it's morphine again, say it's
bad. Then go and make coffee. Black and strong, a
lot of it.'

Liesl could not take her eyes from the pale face
lolling helplessly on the pillow. He looked like a half-
collapsed rag doll being subjected to some humiliating
make-believe in a child's game. 'He has killed
himself!' she said in a whisper. 'So he did do it! The
poor boy!'

It was what they would all say, but Susan had no
time to argue. She shouted furiously over her

shoulder: 'Get the doctor, I said!' and turned a face of such passionate rage that Liesl jumped and ran to obey.

Susan took Laurence's limp body by the shoulders, and shook him until the uncontrolled quakings of the dangling head brought a rush of tears to her eyes, and made her stop for fear he should be jolted to pieces. She thrust her hands under his armpits and hauled him up in the bed, and taking his dead weight into her arms, shook and coaxed and called him by his name in a voice of hopeless exasperation, but for all the effect it had she might have been embracing his pillow. She eased him back gently to lean against the headboard, so that she might have both hands free, and began to slap his livid cheeks, first lightly, then harder, and at last in her desperation with vicious slaps that cracked like whips. The poor abused head rolled defencelessly on the raised pillow, his fair hair tumbling over his forehead, and the marks of her fingers began to stain his cheeks a hectic red beneath the blue pits of his eyes. He gave no sign of feeling either movement or pain; she was the one who winced at every blow, and wept impotently as she belaboured him.

'Oh, poor Laurence!' she said piteously. 'Poor darling!' But she did not stop slapping him until her eyes fell on the pitcher of cold water on his washstand. She wet the end of a towel in it, wrung it out, and began to flick him in the face with that, and it seemed to her that at the shock of the cold the skin round his mouth did quiver and contract. Encouraged, she went on with her devoted cruelties. Presently she thought he drew a slight, wincing, gasp that broke the long, snoring rhythm of his breathing, but she wanted it so much that she was afraid to believe in it, and she dared not stop her efforts for a moment. It felt to her as if she had spent an hour at least in ill-using him, but in reality it was only five minutes.

She was bathed in sweat by the time the doctor flung open the door and erupted into the room like a small grey whirlwind, his bag under his arm. She had forgotten that he would have to get it out of the safe, and probably had had to rouse Franz to obtain the key. At least he had taken her word for it, and not waited to make sure that he was not being fetched out of bed on a fool's errand.

He took one look over her shoulder, patted her back, and said briefly: 'Keep going, you're on the right lines.'

She heard him moving about at her back, heard the small clatter of instruments on the table, but she did not look round. Someone else had come in, too, she thought it must be Franz by the length and loudness of the step. Obstinately, with tears running unheeded down her cheeks, she wet the towel again, and went on with her work.

Something was happening at last. The faintest sounds of protest, little whimpers and gasps of pain, began to catch at his long-drawn breaths and shiver them to pieces. Tremors contorted the smooth skin of his forehead, jerking his brows together as the blows fell, but as soon as she took heart and let him rest for a moment his forehead smoothed out again into marble indifference, and the awful iron sequence resumed its long-drawn in and out. Every time she thought she had drawn him almost to the surface he slipped through her fingers again and sank.

'Wake up, you devil!' she hissed at him, and laid her wet cheek against his hot one for a moment, and uttered a cry of delight at hearing him sigh.

'All right, girl, all right,' said the doctor gently, coming to the other side of the bed. 'Let the poor lad rest for a minute, and sit back out of my light.'

She sat back obediently on her heels and watched the examination anxiously.

'Pulse could be worse. Not breathing too badly.' He lifted one of the heavy eyelids with a fingertip, and frowned at the blind stare of the shrunken pupil. 'He's tougher than you think, girl, don't look so desperate. Come on, help me to turn him over.'

She slid an arm under Laurence's shoulders, and lifted him, but Franz stepped forward and took him from her. The light weight was nothing to him, it was like handling a baby.

Susan looked up across the bed at the hypodermic in the doctor's hand. 'What is it?' she demanded, on a sharp note of challenge and fear.

'Emetic. And drastic. No choice about it, I haven't the means to get rid of it with less strain on him. This is going to be no pretty bit of pillow-smoothing. If you want to leave him to us now, do.' But he knew she wouldn't; it would have surprised him very much if she had moved tamely away from the bed. 'Wonder how long he's had the stuff in him. Do you know?'

She looked at the little oval tray on the bedside table, with its glass tumbler in a metal cup, the handle wrapped in a paper napkin. 'A long time, I'm afraid. It must have been in the wine. Liesl says about eleven. Can you— Will he be all right?'

The needle went in and Laurence never flinched.

'Can't tell yet. It's going to be a fight. We'll have a better idea if this works.' And he hoisted Laurence over again on to his back, and propped him upright against the headboard, drawing the quilt up round him. 'Better let Franz take him, he'll be heavy for you.'

'No,' she said, and laid the cold, wet towel on his clammy forehead and cheeks, and again saw the blue lips contract. 'No, I can manage him.'

She dared not leave him. How could she? Someone had tried to kill him, and she did not know who. She felt that the doctor was fighting for him as she was, but even her own instincts she could not trust. What could he do but fight, once he was called to a desperate case? To do less than his most obstinate best was to be suspect at once. Even his own professional habits of mind would drive him to make a good job of it, once there was no help for it. No, she held her ground in the only way she reasonably could, by rising to the occasion. If she cried, if she was clumsy or inadequate, they would have an excuse to throw her out, and if they threw her out Laurence would die.

She had him more than halfway to consciousness by the time the convulsions of nausea stiffened the cords of his throat and tore at the muscles of his body. She braced her knee on the edge of the bed and slid her arm down over his shoulder and across his breast, and let his limp weight lie forward over it, steadying his forehead in her other hand. Her arms ached, but they held him. The spasms of agonising sickness came in waves, shaking her no less than him. For the first time his sleep was really broken, and between the throes he managed to swallow

153

draughts of a warm, weak solution the doctor presented to his lips. She didn't have to ask about that, she recognised it by its colour as permanganate of potash, which seemed inexplicable, but at this pale strength certainly innocuous.

In the paroxysms, which continued for some time, he fought for breath, sobbing, and she felt movements of his eyelids, and the muscles of his temples and brows, wonderful and grateful in the palm of her hand, and the labouring of his chest upon her arm; movements for the first time originating with him, instead of with her. She was only afraid that the awful retching would go on to the point of exhaustion, and kill him by another way; but it passed, and he hung inert over her arm, half conscious but too weak to try to raise himself. She sat down on the edge of the bed, and hoisted him into the hollow of her shoulder, and used the wet towel to wipe his cold, damp brow and bitter lips.

'That's better,' said Dr Randall approvingly, waving Franz and the bowl away from the bed. 'Responded like an angel. Couldn't have a better patient.' He took Laurence's chin in his hand and turned the drained face to the light, and the eyes, half-opened, tried to focus on him for a moment before the lids came wearily down over them again. 'Oh, no, you don't! Now you're here you'll stay here, my lad, even if you don't find it very comfortable. Come on, now, let's get a stimulant into you, you're going to need it before we're done with you.' He looked at Susan across the bed, and found time for a smile. 'Methylamphetamine,' he said before she could ask. 'Any wiser? You can look it up afterwards. It's only thanks to an awkward post-operative case

I happen to have it with me. Wish I had leptazol, but I haven't. But we'll give him a shot of dextrose, too, while we're about it.'

The needle again, and this time Laurence was aware of it, even if it meant nothing to him except the invasion of his sleep. His skin jerked protestingly at the pricks, his sour mouth gasped into the pillow.

'No, I know you don't like it,' said the doctor almost gaily, 'but you're not being consulted. Curse all you like, it won't hurt you, and it'll encourage me. Now come along, help yourself a little. Turn over, like a good boy, and sit up nicely.' He had no choice, he was lifted briskly back to his old position, propped up on Susan's shoulder, and settled there like an infant being dumped in his high chair. 'Now, Mehlert, where's that coffee your girl promised us? We might get some of it down him now.'

'Ready!' said Liesl's voice eagerly from the doorway, where she must have been standing motionless for some time if anyone had had leisure to notice her; and she was off like a flash to fetch it, glad to be doing something useful at last. Neil was there, too, standing quite still beside the wall, out of everyone's way, waiting until he should be needed. Susan had never noticed when he appeared, and felt obscurely grateful for his restraint, which had taken such care not to disturb her frenzied concentration. Miranda, thank God, must have slept through everything. They had made very little noise throughout, with luck she need know nothing until the danger was past.

Liesl brought a large pot of coffee, black and steaming. The doctor took Laurence by the chin again, and shook him briskly, for his eyelids had already closed. He frowned and tried to jerk himself away; it was a feeble effort, but the resentment that inspired it almost brought a round of applause.

'That's a bit more like the sweet-tempered child we know,' said the doctor, delighted, and cracked him sharply on the cheek. The shock brought him back to the surface and opened his eyes wide in staring reproach, though it was still questionable if he saw anything or anyone distinctly. Before he could sink again the cup was at his lips, and with frequent nudges and shakings and much hectoring they kept him hard at work swallowing down coffee until he let his head fall back exhausted onto Susan's shoulder, and panted for breath. And even when the others let him rest she was at him, hunching her shoulder to jog him awake again every time sleep came near, mopping the cold sweat from his forehead and the spilled coffee from his pyjamas and the quilt, and gently wiping his mouth after his shaky efforts to oblige them and get them to let him alone.

'He's a better colour,' she said, but it was rather an appeal to the doctor to agree with her than a genuine statement of opinion.

'He's breathing quite nicely. If we can keep him awake I think he'll be all right, but it's going to be a long business. You girls had better go and get some sleep.'

Liesl went meekly back to bed when her father told her to go; someone had to be ready to go ahead with the work in the morning. But Susan stared back defiantly and did not move.

'All right, you obstinate female,' said the doctor, without displeasure, 'feed him some more coffee.'

156

She did it somewhat better singlehanded, taking her time, and he was beginning to understand what was demanded of him, and to respond automatically by sipping and swallowing every time she shook him. It was a slow business, holding him in one arm and alternately feeding him and mopping him up with the other. Good practice for future motherhood, she thought bitterly, and no longer marvelled that small children sometimes get smacked out of sheer impatience.

'Pulse is coming along nicely,' said Dr Randall approvingly, 'heart quite strong. He's really behaving very well. I don't think there's much fear of a collapse. Come on, young man, I think it's time we got you on your feet.'

When they dragged him out of bed he spoke for the first time, saying the thing he was to say over and over before the night was out. His lips and tongue would not move freely, and all that emerged was a trailing thread of sound, but they heard and understood it. 'Oh, God!' he said entreatingly, 'leave me alone!' But they took no notice of him. They put his slippers on his feet, and got him by force into his dressing gown, and the doctor held him about the body and drew one limp arm round his own lean middle-aged neck, and hauled the boy upright. Susan was glad that he was too absorbed to delegate the job to Neil and Franz, for now she, the only one present of a comparable height with the doctor, was able to fall in unchallenged on the other side.

At first they dragged him bodily from end to end of the little room, his helpless feet trailing pathetically. They bullied and jolted him at every step without mercy, shook him, coaxed him, threatened him, until even having to hear the constant flow of their voices was like being beaten. His head lolled on the doctor's shoulder and was roughly shaken erect. It declined wearily upon Susan's and she heaved it off with a jerk that bruised his cheekbone unpleasantly. He had to do what they wanted, just to get some peace. He had to do it, whatever it was, reasonable or unreasonable. They kept nagging at him to walk, to stand up, to come on. He began to force his feeble muscles and sleepy brain to obey, because if he didn't they would never let him alone. But he gave in and did as they told him, and still they didn't let him alone.

'So tired,' he said, mumbling piteously against Susan's hair. 'Want to lie down – please—!' But the more words he managed to get out intact, the more heartlessly they dragged him up and down the room, and nothing he said would ever move them, and nothing he did would ever appease them. He began to hate them all, long before he had any clear idea who they were.

'I know you're tired. So are we. But you've got to go on. Come on, be a good boy, it's for your own good.' How often he'd heard that in his life, and always for detestable things which had never, as far as he could see, done him a particle of good.

'I can't! Oh, leave me alone!' He would have cried if he'd had the necessary strength left. He would have gone on his knees to them and begged for mercy, if they had not held him pitilessly upright.

'Darling, we can't leave you alone, you've got to keep moving. You mustn't go to sleep, not yet. Later on you shall sleep, I promise you. Come along, do as we ask you.'

And he did, because he had no choice. He supposed vaguely, for a moment, that it must be his mother there on his left, though it was a long time since she'd called him darling. Still, it was just like her to couple the endearment with an inflexible command to something he didn't want to do.

'I'm thirsty,' he said plaintively. Ideas were connecting in his reviving brain. It was almost certainly night. Night and his mother's presence used to be good for a drink between them, and a drink must mean a pause, leave to sit down. They let him sink on to the edge of the bed, and supported him while he drank a whole cup of strong, sweet coffee, and for some reason they were pleased with him. He was at a loss to know why. As soon as they took their hands from him for a moment to put the cup out of harm's way his eyelids sank, and he bowed forward thankfully into Susan's lap; and for one moment she gathered his rumpled head to her and cried over him, but the next moment she lifted him brusquely, and shook him awake.

'No! Come on, get up! Do you hear? On your feet! You can't sleep yet.'

When Susan and the doctor tired Neil and Franz took over. That was better for Laurence, Susan had to admit; they were taller than he was, instead of somewhat shorter, and being held higher gave him better control of his unsteady legs. But for her it was infinitely worse. To be occupied with him was one thing, but to sit pressed into a corner of the room and watch him dragged endlessly up and down by others, whimpering with exhaustion and begging despairingly to be let alone, was quite another. And it went on and on, without respite. The winter daylight came, frosty and bright, and still they walked him relentlessly from end to end of his room.

Those who had spent the night normally began to awake and get up. Trevor, having heard the news from Liesl, came quietly in with a wary face and concerned eyes, and breathed again at sight of the drooping victim in unwilling but undoubted action. Like a considerate person, as he was, he shouldered the burden of encountering Mrs Quayne, and went off to keep careful watch for her appearance and ward her off from the sickroom. McHugh came, too, large and startled and constrained, and offered to relieve Franz. He looked fresh and vigorous as ever, and yet he had probably come back from the village only about two hours ago, just in time to avoid the light. Something of the glossy complacency of his triumph was still visible on him; and he was unexpectedly kind in his handling of the poor tormented soul who hung limply upon his shoulder.

'Go and get some breakfast, Everard, I can manage him alone for a bit. Come on, sonny, put your weight on Mac, he won't let you down.'

He handled him buoyantly and bracingly, jockeying him along step by step, even singing to him by moments in the lightness of his heart. It was better for the victim to be in the hands of someone who cared less about him, thought Susan, someone whose kindness was a simple overflow from his own sense of abundant well-being, a bonus he could spare for the less fortunate, since he had neither the means nor the temperament to store it for his own use. She sat and watched them together, though she had been told to go and eat, and she could well afford to go and leave him in McHugh's care. Of all people, she had no reason now to suspect McHugh; that was finished. He had been alone in his room long before Liesl heated the wine at eleven, and he had left his room only to go straight to his rendezvous with Frau Agathe. Whatever mischief he had done during his brief stay in Oberschwandegg, he had certainly not poisoned Laurence; and the inescapable inference was that he had not killed Richard Hellier, either. She was back at the beginning again; but at least there could be a beginning. Laurence was alive.

'And this has been going on all night?' said McHugh. 'How come I never heard a thing?'

'You wouldn't,' she said, 'at that distance.' It was the first time she had felt like smiling, and even now it was a wry smile. 'We didn't make any noise about it, where was the good?'

'Poor chap, he's just about clinched the case against himself. Almost seems a pity you didn't let him get away with it. Look what he's still got to go through!'

There it was again, the inevitable assumption of suicide. But at least McHugh was not himself the murderer, reproaching them for keeping Laurence alive because his own plans had thereby been spoiled. His compassion, if mistaken, was genuine. She was spared the necessity of loathing him.

'Why don't you go and rest? He's surely going to be all right now.'

'Not until the doctor says he's safe.'

Dr Randall came back from the kitchen bearing a tray with fresh coffee and a small bowl of eggs and milk laced with brandy.

'All right, girl, he'll do now. Don't worry, the worst's over. Make the bed for him, and we'll get him into it and spoon some food into him. Come on, old boy, we won't torment you any more.'

They propped him up on his pillows, and Susan fed him like a baby, and whatever she offered him he took docilely, too broken to put up any resistance; but faint colour had come back into his face, the blue shadows had faded perceptibly from round eyes and mouth, and he was breathing naturally. As yet he knew none of them as persons, they were only incomprehensible forces disposing of him against his will.

'I'll give him another shot, to be on the safe side. Don't worry about him any more, he's going to be all right. Right as rain by tomorrow.'

They eased him down in the bed and covered him warmly. The drooping eyelids had already closed gratefully, the worn face was smoothing out into a wonderful tranquillity.

'He's asleep already,' said Susan with a tremor of fear.

'That isn't morphine, that's just plain exhaustion. Pulse is firm as a rock. He needs sleep, as long as it's proper sleep. Think of the hell of a night he's had.'

She looked up across the sleeper into the doctor's face, and said very deliberately: 'He didn't try to kill himself, you know.'

'Have I said he did?'

'No, you haven't said it. But that's what you're thinking.'

'Never believe you can tell from this face of mine what I'm thinking,' he said placidly. 'I've been around the world too long for that.' He drew the covers closer over Laurence's shoulders, and took Susan by the arm. 'Come on, you've got to eat something, and then get some rest. I'll be around to look after him while you sleep.'

They followed McHugh from the room.

'Lock the door,' said Susan, halting firmly in the corridor.

He looked at her without surprise, but he asked gently: 'Why? Because he's just confirmed the general opinion that he's a murderer found out?'

'Because someone tried to murder him,' said Susan, 'and even now he may try again.'

CHAPTER XII

Has bitter wrong, a sinful deed been done?
                                                    Act 3

'He did not try to kill himself,' said Susan for the
third time, and clenched her fists on the edge of the
table.

They were all there, all except the sleeper upstairs.
Dr Randall and McHugh sat one on either side of her,
Neil and Trevor faced her across the table, with
Miranda between them, still red-eyed from her visit
to her son. The doctor had cut the permitted time
to a few minutes, and firmly restrained her from
disturbing the patient's rest. She had had to play her
scene in silence.

'My dear girl,' said Trevor gently, 'Randall has told
us that this was morphine again, beyond any doubt.
You know as well as we do where the phial that held
the morphine tablets was found. I'm sorry, but
there's no getting away from it. Only two tablets
were found in it. The rest he must have had
concealed somewhere else, against emergencies.
Randall said at the time that half the amount missing
could have accounted for Richard. The dose
Laurence took can't possibly have come from any
other source than those same tablets. Who else in this
place would have morphine? No, it's pretty clear

that the remaining tablets were hidden, well hidden, somewhere in his room. When he knew that the police would probably be able to get here today, or at the latest tomorrow—'

'Did he know it? Why should he? He was a prisoner in his room, he never heard us discussing it.'

'I'm afraid he did know,' Neil said quietly. 'Franz mentioned it to him.'

She shrugged it off impatiently. 'I don't know why I even asked the question, it doesn't matter whether he knew or not. He did not take the morphine himself, because he didn't have it, and he didn't have it because he never stole it from Dr Randall's bag. He did not try to kill himself, because he had done nothing to make him want a way out.'

Miranda had opened her mouth twice, ready to spring to her son's defence, and twice found herself unable to speak. Now sheer astonishment silenced her. She sat staring across the table at Susan over her handkerchief, and managed at last in a dazed voice: 'But you – it was you—'

'I started it. Yes, I know I did, but for a reason. What I've got to say now I've already told to Neil, and now I'm telling you all, and you'd better listen. Laurence never stole any morphine, never thought for a moment of hurting Richard. When it was suggested that his fingerprints on the glass were strong evidence against him I let you all go on thinking so. I encouraged you to think so. But only because I thought the real criminal might give himself away by trying to plant more evidence on him. I made a horrible mistake, and somehow that evidence was planted successfully without my knowledge, and made you decide quite definitely that Laurence was guilty. But he isn't. I can swear to that, and I shall swear to it, and nothing's going to shake me. From the time when that glass of brandy was placed on Richard's table until midnight, when we found Richard dead, Laurence was with me. On the only occasion when he approached that table I had him clearly in view, and the glass, too, every moment of the time. He neither touched it nor dropped anything into it. Yesterday I told Neil that, but I didn't make it public because of warning the murderer. But I have reason to believe that at least two more people overheard us talking. And last night someone tried to kill Laurence.'

Several gasps of protest interrupted her, but she rode over them.

'Someone tried to kill Laurence. You all heard what Trevor just said: Laurence tried to commit suicide because he knew himself a murderer found out, and saw no way of escape when the police got here. That's what all of you were thinking, except his mother. That's what you were meant to think, what the police were meant to think. Well, now you can think again! I've told you now that he never killed anybody, and never thought of killing himself. I tell you so, all of you, and I'm going to tell Herr Mehlert and his wife and Liesl, so that if there's any second attempt on Laurence's life you'll all know the reason. And the police will know it, however soon or however late they come, I'll make sure of that. In fact, I'm serving notice on one of you, here and now, to *leave Laurence alone*!'

Susan was on her feet before the end of it, colour flaming in her face. A stupefied silence saluted her climax, a satisfying silence because it was full of understanding. No one could pretend to misunderstand.

No one but a madman could ignore the warning, after that. If a finger was laid on Laurence now, her story was confirmed beyond reasonable doubt. If she was right, if the murderer had tried to clinch the case by making it appear that the culprit had put an end to himself in despair, from now on he must make the best of his failure. To try a second time was to damn himself and vindicate her. Laurence hurt again was Laurence proved innocent.

Dr Randall was the first to get his breath back. He looked up at her with a gleam in his eyes, and said appreciatively: 'Girl, that was really telling 'em!'

Trevor said, with something less than his usual calm: 'Do I understand that you're making an accusation against one of us here, Susan?'

'Whether you understand it is up to you. I'm making it. Against whichever of you here poisoned Richard and tried to poison Laurence. Whoever he is, he knows. I don't. If I did, I'd tell you.'

There was a brief pause, and then Neil said steadily: 'Since this is all coming into the open now, I'd better tell you what I said to Susan when she told me this yesterday. I told her that I didn't feel able on the spur of the moment either to accept or reject her story. I said that where the same person told two opposing stories on two consecutive days she made it very difficult indeed for anyone to accept either of them unreservedly. But I also advised her not to repeat what she'd said to anyone else, in order not to put the murderer on guard, *if* she was now telling the truth. I said I should keep a faithful record of everything, and hand it over to the police as soon as that became possible, and that it would be for them to proceed on the evidence, not for me – thank

God! I don't see what else I could have done, and I thought I was wronging no one. I didn't anticipate either that Laurence would feel desperate enough for suicide, or that the murderer – assuming him to be someone other than Laurence – would conceive the idea of killing him to establish his guilt beyond question. More particularly, I didn't think he would have the opportunity, even if he conceived the idea. It seemed to me that Laurence, where he was, was the safest of the lot of us. No one but Franz took food in to him, it looked absolutely foolproof. But since this horrible thing has happened, suicide attempt or murder attempt, whichever it may be, we're obliged to examine the circumstances.' '

'Now you're talking,' said Susan, and sat down again.

'In that case,' said Dr Randall, 'it might be as well if I made a rough statement on the spot. There'll be no second attempt on Laurence by himself or anyone else, at least not by poison – not only because in the latter case it would be extremely stupid on the murderer's part, as Susan has pointed out, but also because the supply has now run out. I think you may safely say that Laurence took all that was left over from Richard's dose. Apart, of course, from the two we found in the phial. Those are now locked in the safe. So is my bag, and even in emergencies it won't be touched again except with Franz standing by as a witness. So no more poison is available to our hypothetical enemy. I thought you might like to have that clear, for your reassurance. Laurence had the lion's share, I fancy, but he happens to be a very tough young man, with excellent resistance – otherwise he wouldn't be with us now. Also he had the luck to be found in time. He had a drink late at night, I understand about eleven. There's very little doubt that the papaveretum was taken with, or in, that. If he'd swallowed it earlier, with his dinner, we should have been too late to save him. Now if the dose was self-administered there should not, I think, be any traces of it in the dregs of the spiced wine. When you're taking tablets you simply put them on your tongue and take a drink to wash them down. But if you want to administer them to someone else you dissolve them in liquid or hide them in food. And if examination of the wine tumbler does reveal traces of morphine, then Susan is right, and this was attempted murder.'

He spread his thin fingers on the table, and smiled round upon them all from under his bushy brows. 'The tumbler, I need hardly say, is in the safe with the rest of the material evidence. And now I think it remains for us to hear from Liesl and Herr Mehlert the exact history of that drink.'

'I'll ask them to come,' said Neil, rising.

Liesl came in from the kitchen wiping her hands on her embroidered apron, and told her brief story in English.

'Dr Randall went to see the young gentleman with my father when he took him his dinner, and when they came down he said that Mr Quayne had a cold, and perhaps at bedtime I should spice some wine for him. We were a little late, because Herr Kerner and Fritzi came again to see to Mr Hellier – you understand,' she explained hesitantly, 'Herr Kerner is making the coffin. So I spiced wine for them, too, and when I was ready – I think it was just a few minutes before eleven – I brought out the two trays from the kitchen—'

'Wait a moment,' said Neil. 'Did anyone come into the kitchen to you while you were heating the wine?'

'No, no one.'

'And you didn't leave it at all?'

'Not at all. So the tray with the glasses for Herr Kerner and Fritzi I carried into the bar, where my father was sitting talking with them. But because I had no hand free to open the door I put down the young gentleman's tray on the table close to the foot of the stairs, there in the hall.'

'And left it there while you went into the bar?'

'Yes,' she said, looking frightened at the thought.

'But that would be only for a moment. You didn't close the door of the bar?'

'Yes, I did. You see, when my father is talking to Herr Kerner he goes on talking, they both go on talking, sometimes for a long time. And I could not take up the tray myself, he would not let me. I called to him as soon as I opened the door: "Father, Mr Quayne's tray is ready," but he went on talking. So I went in to them and said it again, and he said: "Yes, I'm coming," but he did not come at once. And I did not want the wine to get cold, so I went on saying it until he did go and take it upstairs.'

'And how long would that be?'

'Not very long. I think perhaps three minutes, maybe four.'

'And then,' said Neil to Franz, 'you took it straight to him in his room, and locked him in again with it? No one else met you on the way?'

'No one. The young man was already in bed, but awake. He began to drink the wine at once.'

'But you didn't see him drink the whole of it? You didn't wait?'

'No, I gave it to him and came away.'

'So he could have got out of bed and unearthed the tablets from some hiding place after he was alone. But equally there seems to be a period of three or four minutes when the tray stood on the hall table, and anyone could have meddled with it. Liesl, you didn't hear anyone moving in the hall during those few minutes?'

'I am sorry,' she said sadly. 'We were all talking in the bar. Anyone could have passed through. Though I think some were already in bed. I remember Miss Conroy went early to bed – and Mr McHugh—'

'Yes. Thank you, both, I think that's all.' And when they were gone he went on soberly: 'Of course, there was nothing to prevent the early birds from coming down again. The house is quiet enough after about half-past ten, you can wander around without being much troubled with company. It looks as if all have to account for ourselves for, say, ten minutes before and ten minutes after eleven o'clock, to allow for some slight inaccuracy in fixing the time. To begin with myself – I hadn't gone to bed, but I was in my room from about half-past ten, and I didn't leave it again. Mrs Quayne?'

'I was in bed by ten,' she said stiffly. 'Though you can hardly suppose in any case that I should want to hurt my own son.'

But couldn't you? Not in any circumstances? Mothers have killed their children before now, and children their mothers. Susan shivered, and pushed the intolerable thought away from her. No, it was ridiculous. Richard she might have murdered for money; but if she had, the thing would have been done as much for Laurence as for herself. She would never have wanted to harm her son, her unlucky aptitude was only for harming him without wanting to. She did love him, however she had cramped his life. She *did* love him, didn't she?

'Trevor?'

'I was in the bar earlier in the evening. I left about twenty to eleven. It gets boring after the locals leave. At eleven I was in the bath,' said Trevor calmly, 'so you can hardly expect me to provide a witness.'

'Randall?'

'I came upstairs just after Mason, I can vouch for him as far as his own door, and I think the time he's quoted you is about right. I'd been in here reading since dinner. I was in bed just before eleven.'

'McHugh?'

Susan had forgotten the implications the question might have for McHugh, even though he had no need to lie. He smiled to himself with remembered pleasure as he said cheerfully: 'I was in bed, too. Model household, weren't we? I went off to my room about ten o'clock.'

'Susan?'

'So did I, almost immediately after Mr McHugh. I left the bar only a minute or so later.'

'And nobody heard or saw any movements about the house later, around eleven?'

Silence answered this query, an alert, reserved silence while everyone covertly observed his neighbours.

'Then, quite simply, any one of us might have gone downstairs again and doctored the wine. None of us can be reckoned clear of suspicion. And equally Laurence may very well have made use of the tablets himself within his own room. Susan's argument that a second attack could not possibly be passed off as a suicide attempt is sound enough, but purely speculative. We're concerned only with what has happened, not with what may happen in the future. And what has happened could still have been Laurence's own doing. For all I know the police may still prefer that explanation to any other. At any rate, it's up to them, all we can do is render a full report, and a true one, and that we shall do.' Neil stood up, pushing back his chair. 'Personally, I'm now going to help with the digging. By tonight I hope the track will be open.'

'Good idea!' McHugh came to his feet gaily. 'I'll come with you. Might as well make ourselves useful.'

Trevor did not offer to accompany them. Digging a way through frozen snow between enclosing rocks was not in his line, however much he longed to escape from Oberschwandegg. As for the doctor, he went back to his sleeping patient, so promptly that Susan plucked at his sleeve to ask him anxiously: 'He is out of danger, isn't he?'

'Oh, yes, he'll be all right now, he's over it. I just want to stand by for a few hours in case he still needs a stimulant.'

'Can I come and sit with him? Just until lunch? You could get a few hours' rest, and I could sleep later. I'd call you if he woke up, or if there seemed anything wrong.'

'Girl, you're crazy! And I've just sidetracked his mother by telling her I was going to sit with him myself.' But he let her into the room perforce, since he was sure even if he ordered her away she would not go.

174

Laurence was sleeping with the abandon of a child exhausted, his face burrowing deeply into the pillow. Susan drew a chair close to the bed, and kept guard over him through what was left of the morning, until the savoury smells of Frau Mehlert's cooking and the big, hearty voices of the returning labourers announced the approach of lunchtime. He did not move when the doctor came in again, refreshed, shaven, and fed, and sent Susan down to her meal, nor had he stirred when she returned.

Neil came in for a few minutes before he went back to his digging. He sat down on the opposite side of the bed, and stared thoughtfully and rather miserably at the drawn face on the pillow.

'You know what nobody remembered to ask you, Susan?' He kept his voice very low, not to trouble the sleeper. 'What were you doing up and fully dressed in the middle of the night?' He lifted to her a brief and intimate smile, foreseeing what her answer would be.

'I hadn't been to bed. I was waiting and trying to get up my courage to go and talk to him. I wanted to tell him why I'd pitched him into this horrible position, and to say that of course I meant to tell the truth and get him out of it again. But the first time I tried it I didn't carry any more conviction with him than I did with you,' she said bitterly, 'only in another way, and I don't suppose I should have done any better last night, either. As it turned out it didn't arise. I couldn't get any answer from him. So I roused Liesl, and made her come with me to see if he was all right.'

'Lucky for him!' said Neil. 'You be careful this unknown murderer of yours doesn't turn nasty with you, my girl. You've thrown a fair-sized spanner into the works for him, you know.' He grinned at her, not unkindly. He could afford to grin at the conception, she thought wryly, since he didn't believe in it. He was still sure that the murderer was here between them in the bed, sleeping like a baby.

The doctor turned back the coffee-stained sheet to reach for Laurence's wrist. 'Nice, steady pulse,' he said contentedly. 'Let's see if I can sound his heart without disturbing him. I think he might be the better for one more dextrose injection, last night took a lot out of him.'

Under his ministrations Laurence stirred and sighed, and the deep, long breaths stilled into quietness. He shivered lightly, and turned on his back, and lay with closed eyes, frowning and moistening his dry lips, on which the bitter after-taste of nausea lingered unpleasantly.

'Thirsty!' he muttered, his face contorting in sour distaste.

Susan reached for the jug of lemonade Liesl had provided, poured a glassful, and slid her right arm under him to raise him while he drank. Neil encircled him from the other side, and took his weight from her. The heavy lids, still blue-stained and underlined with shadows, opened slowly upon dazed hazel eyes, and his lips parted eagerly and leaned to drink. Then, as though he had recognized first the hand that held the glass, his labouring glance climbed her arm and arrived at her face.

He stared for a moment with drawn brows, while colour came back into his cheeks and sharp and painful intelligence into his eyes; then deliberately and arrogantly he drew back his head and turned his face away from her into Neil's shoulder.

She felt Neil's startled eyes upon her for an instant in embarrassment and pity before he hastily averted them. Dr Randall, who was preparing his syringe at the table, had turned his head and was staring at them sharply. She sat for a moment, frozen into stillness, and then with fastidious care withdrew her arm, leaving Neil to support the invalid who had so pointedly rejected her. She held out the glass across the bed, and Neil took it from her without venturing to meet her eyes. From him Laurence accepted the offering greedily, and drank and drank until he had all but emptied the glass. She did not wait to see it, however, the door had already closed quietly upon her departure. She took her dignity with her unimpaired to the privacy of her own room, if that was any satisfaction to her. That door, too, closed upon her without emphasis. Laurence had done what Dr Randall could not manage, and sent her to bed at last.

Neil, setting the glass back on the tray, raised a significant eyebrow at the doctor, and laid his burden gently back into the pillows. 'I think,' said he, 'I'd better get back to work.' His look and his faintly embarrassed, faintly dismayed grin said plainly: 'Digging is less complicated.'

After he had left the room the silence was almost oppressive. Laurence had stung himself into complete wakefulness with that decisive act of rejection, and a certain hypersensitivity warned him that he was the object of marked disapproval, though he was completely at sea about everything else. He lay breathing rather quickly, flags of rising colour in his cheeks, his eyes fixed defensively on the doctor's face; but all the doctor said, very drily, was: 'Turn over!'

It was extraordinary what unquestionable authority doctors had, as soon as you were in their hands, even if you had very little idea of how you had got there. Laurence turned obediently on his face. The needle went in with a vicious jab which hurt, and perhaps had been meant to hurt. It jerked an indignant gasp out of him, and made him turn his head just far enough to train one amazed and reproachful eye upon the doctor's face.

'Young man,' said the doctor grimly, returning the look, 'if you were in your usual rude health I'd give you something more than a few needle pricks to feel sore about. All right, you can turn over again now.' And when his patient had righted himself and settled back defiantly into his pillow, Dr Randall sat down on the edge of his bed and fixed him with severe eyes. 'Aren't you ashamed of yourself?'

'No,' said Laurence, smouldering.

'You will be when I've finished with you.' The doctor took a deep breath, and began to talk. The entire history of Laurence's lost night took no more than three minutes to tell, and submerged recollections of misery and indignity rose out of his cloudy memory to fuse with what he heard. His eyes, fixed in fascination on the doctor's face, grew larger and wider as he listened. 'And then,' said the doctor warmly, 'you wake up and slap her in the face like that, a girl who's fought for you all night like a tigress. And you say you're not ashamed of yourself! You should have heard her tearing into us downstairs on your behalf, my lad. Oh, no, you don't! You lie down again, I haven't told you you can get out of bed.'

He took his agitated patient by the shoulders, and tucked him back into bed without much trouble; his strength was not yet equal to his will, and even this slight effort had brought out drops of sweat on his forehead.

'I've got to talk to her,' said Laurence feverishly. 'I didn't know – Oh, God, can't you see I *must* see her?'

'So you shall, but not yet. You're going to calm down and eat some lunch, and put in several more hours sleeping, and then we'll see about asking Susan if she'll condescend to look in on you again.'

'But it was so horrible, what I did. Suppose she won't come near me? Please let me go to her now, just for a moment, only to apologise, only to tell her—'

'Let me catch you trying to budge from this bed, and you'll be even sorrier for yourself than you were last night. By this evening you may be fit to get on your legs for a bit. You can just live with your ungrateful young self for a few hours more, like it or lump it. You don't deserve any better.' But the tone of his voice had warmed considerably; he was well pleased with his penitent.

Laurence lay back flushed and large-eyed. 'And she's come right out and told everybody I didn't do it? She never really believed I had? She— Damn, and now I've made her think badly of me, after all. Oh, God, I could kick myself!'

'That's an idea,' said the doctor. 'You do that.'

'But I couldn't very well know, could I? It wasn't all my fault. It hurt like hell, thinking she— And then she did all that for me!' An obscure memory rose out of the darkness of his lost hours, when death had fought to keep its hold of him, as Susan had fought to break it. 'You know, I could have sworn someone called me – I don't remember very much, but I thought somebody said "Darling" – twice! But she couldn't have, could she?'

'Why not?' said the doctor, still moved to administer a judicious back-hander here and there. 'If her pet dog was ill she'd call him that. I daresay you got in by the back door of womanly sympathy, too.' But the wide, wondering stare took no account of this cold douche. Laurence reached out and caught at his hand; the hot, trembling clasp of the long fingers startled and moved him.

'Won't you please go and ask her to come to me just for a moment? Say I'm terribly sorry, I didn't know what I was doing. Say I beg her to come.'

In the end he had to go, in order to calm his patient down; but he came back empty-handed.

'Now listen to me, young man. You can't see her now, because she's in bed and fast asleep, and if anyone needs it, she does. I expect she crept into bed to cry in private over you, you ungrateful brat, but she'd be asleep almost as soon as she lay down. She's plain exhausted. I promise you shall see her as soon as she gets up again, but I'm not going to wake her for you or anyone. You've got nothing to worry about, boy, she'll be ready to listen. Now, are you going to behave yourself and do as I tell you?'

Laurence, compelled to make do with this, said that he was. It left him plenty to look forward to, at any rate, since all that she had done to him was more than compensated for by all that she had since done for him. The feeling of reconciliation with her was wonderfully sweet to him as he sank again into sleep. Even penitence was not such a bad bedfellow.

CHAPTER XIII

So strangely I'm perplexed,
I would know all things, yet I fear to know
the truth.

Act 3

Susan awoke with a start that set her heart thumping, and lay quivering in the darkness of her room, shaken adrift from place and time. She groped after the past hours, and found no thread to which she could hold. In a silent panic she listened to the low voices outside her door, and was suddenly aware, for no reason, that it was the click of the latch falling into place that had penetrated her sleep.

'She is still asleep.' That was Liesl's voice, in a soft undertone. 'She has not touched her supper tray.'

And Neil answering as softly: 'Surely we could let her sleep on until he's seen all the rest of us. She was so terribly tired. It won't make any difference to him which of us he interviews first.'

A man's voice said something in German, in the broad, resonant voice common to all these mountaineers; but this voice had a tenor quality about it, nonetheless, which did not belong to Franz Mehlert. This was a younger man. She wondered, with straining nerves, who he could be, and did not have long to wonder. 'Herr Klostermann is quite agreeable,' said Liesl. 'We shall call her when she is needed.'

Herr Klostermann – then that grave, burdened young voice belonged to Frau Agathe's husband. But he was below in Bad Schwandegg, how could he be here? Susan lay motionless as the voices receded, while her heart steadied and her mind dragged itself reluctantly from the pit of nothingness where she had taken refuge. Drunk with sleep too long-delayed and too heavy when it came, she could feel at first nothing but gratitude that she had not stirred when Liesl looked into the room; then the troubled memories quickened in her, and in a blinding rush of pain everything came back together, death and sickness and fear, the worst of fears, fear for another. She remembered with terrible clarity Laurence's head heavy on her arm, the long greenish stare of his eyes cold as the snow outside, and his face turning away from her. She had crept away to hide herself, and made far too good a job of it, for now she had lost all the hours between, and the police were here. The road was open, and the party from Bad Schwandegg had broken through the last drift to find murder waiting for them. There was no more time left for thought. Except, of course, that by the mercy of God she had stayed asleep just long enough at the last moment, and she was to be interviewed after all the others. If she could think of a way of being convincing by the time he finished with the rest, Laurence would be safe.

She sat up in bed and looked at her watch. Everything happened by night, the days were for sleeping, so that you could be ready for the feverish acitivity of the darkness. It was just past eleven o'clock, that fatally recurring hour. She had slept for ten hours without a break; she felt as though she had fallen out of the world, and had now to rediscover the technique of moving, thinking, and acting in it, as an injured man learns to walk again.

There was a neat little tray on her bedside table, just as Liesl had said; a vacuum flask of coffee, a little carafe of wine, a covered plate of cold meats and cheeses and pickles, and some buttered biscuits and fruit. They had shown her every possible consideration. Below her in the house, just awakening instead of just falling asleep, she felt rather than heard the big, alien voices of the mountain men, and their long, light footsteps.

She slid her feet out of bed, and pulled on her dressing gown, and stole out into the corridor. From the head of the stairs she could hear clearly the buzz of many voices below, and feel the vibration of excitement that set the air quivering. She crept down to the turn of the stairs, and sat there with her cheek against the wall, hidden from the people who moved restlessly about the hall beneath her.

Neil's voice, authoritatively raised, was explaining above the murmur: 'I'm sorry about this, but it's necessary. He doesn't intend to keep you up any longer than he need, but he wants to interview us all and get a general picture of the case before we call it a day. He wants you all to wait in the dining room until you're called, please.'

The voice that rose highest in protest was, of course, Miranda's, but Trevor, too, seemed to be complaining about being kept from his bed.

'This is a murder case,' Neil reminded them tartly, 'and we're all material witnesses, better bear that in mind. If you're tired, what d'you think Klostermann is? He's spent all day digging his way through to here, only to find he has to go on duty as soon as he gets here, with a vile job like this on his hands. He hasn't even had time to go home and see his wife yet. *You* should grumble!'

They subsided, having no choice. Someone said: 'Susan isn't here. Should we call her?'

'No, let her sleep. He knows about Susan, Liesl will call her when he gets round to her. And Laurence is in his room, of course. Where's McHugh?'

Nobody knew. 'I thought he'd gone to bed, but he hasn't,' said Trevor. 'I looked in to wake him. Maybe he went down to the head of the track again with Franz and the others after dinner, and hasn't hurried back. He had an early night last night, you couldn't expect him to think of turning in before midnight twice running. He'll be along soon.'

'Tell him to stand by, too, when he does come in. I'm going into the office now to hand over all the stuff we've got laid up in the safe.'

The office was a small, quiet back room near the kitchen, and there, it seemed, Klostermann meant to conduct his interviews. Susan heard the door close. The dining-room door must have been left open, for the murmur of subdued, apprehensive voices continued clearly; all English voices there now, the Austrian ones had withdrawn into the kitchen and bar, and the smell of coffee laced with rum came in vagrant waves up the stairs. She sat shivering, but not with cold. In the office the safe would be wide open now. Neil would display every exhibit fastidiously, without touching it, with heartfelt gratitude that he could turn over his unsought responsibility into the proper hands at last. Trevor's photographs, McHugh's masterly collection of finger-prints, the ashtray with the last charred remnants of Richard's will — what talented amateurs we all turned out to be, she thought bitterly, just clever enough to amass a great deal of enigmatic evidence, put it all together and arrive at the wrong answer. And I had to make myself a self-confessed liar right at the start, so that no one should ever again feel sure he could believe me. I was the cleverest of the lot, and the biggest fool. And I'm not so sure I'm grateful to Neil for asking them to let me sleep. At this very moment a picture is being presented which I'm going to find very difficult to refute if I come last. I'd rather have got my blow in first. But he meant it kindly; he's always been kind.

The stab of realisation reached the sensitive part of her mind without warning, and brought her up from the stairs trembling. McHugh was missing from the census! Of all people, McHugh! Thank God no one but she knew where he vanished to in the night. How could he have been so reckless as to go to Frau Agathe so early? She did not want to take away any part of her mind from Laurence, from his wrongs which must be righted, from his innocence which must be defended, and yet other people existed, too, to be hurt unfairly and ruined too lightly. She turned and scurried back to her room and began feverishly to dress, right to her coat and boots. It wasn't for McHugh's sake, damn him, she owed him nothing, but was that poor girl's marriage to be broken in pieces just for his Christmas entertainment? It was too trivial a rock for two lives to founder on, and they, the interlopers, had already done enough damage to Oberschwandegg's immemorial peace. This at least she could ward off in time.

She scribbled a note under the small circle of light her bedside lamp gave. The sealed envelope was addressed to Frau Agathe Klostermann, but on the half-sheet of paper inside it said only, in English: *'Klostermann is here, and on the case. He got through late this evening.'*

McHugh would know the hand; he'd studied the written statements too curiously to fail to recognise it; but what did that matter? She let herself out on to the balcony, and slipped down the wooden stairs into the street, hugging the shadow of the wall, where the broad eaves leaned over her. She did not want to carry the note herself; how could she tell how soon they would send to wake her? But if she must, she must. But as she ran stooping below the dining-room windows the gate of the yard opened, and a man's shambling figure came out. She recognised Fritzi, the elderly innocent who worked for Herr Kerner, the undertaker. Fritzi was never sent away without a cup of coffee and an almond cake from Liesl's tin in the kitchen. Of course, this was the evening on which they were to deliver Richard's coffin; he must be lying in it now, there in his room at the far end of the balcony. Poor Richard, who had suffered the injustice of becoming only a contention and a threat to those who had outlived him.

'Fritzi!' she said softly, and held out to him her letter and a crumpled ten-schilling note. 'For Frau Klostermann – Frau Agathe. *Verstehen Sie?'*

He understood very well; his simple-mindedness did not extend to money. He took the errand in hand with alacrity, nodding his head repeatedly and favouring her with a flood of reassurances which did not even sound like German to her. Delivering the letter would hardly take him out of his own way home, and he was probably entirely reliable.

'Quickly!' she urged, and watched him lope away along the glassy ice of the roadway. The sky was overcast, sagging like lead over the roofs of the houses, and there was a whining, shifting wind. Something too thin and fine-spun to be snow stung her lips. She turned, shivering, and hurried back into the house by the way she had come, and crouched on the staircase again, listening to the voices from below.

How far had they got while she was away? It seemed that Neil was still closeted in the office with Klostermann, for the three voices she heard were those of Trevor, Miranda, and the doctor. Miranda spoke only now and again, fretfully, complaining of her son's usage in tones which indicated that she felt it as an affront to herself rather than an injury to him. Did she really love him at all? Could she love? Supposing she had killed Richard almost on impulse, carried away by an indignation she would feel to be fully justified, and people and events between them had turned the spotlight of suspicion on Laurence, would she let him take the blame for it to save herself? Herself and sixty thousand pounds? Would she even try to clinch the matter by poisoning him, if the need arose? If she were asked that question she would indignantly declare her love for her son, and her willingness rather to suffer for him than to let him suffer for her, and she would mean and believe every word of it. But she wasn't a woman who knew herself very well.

'Motive?' Trevor was saying impatiently. 'Of course Antonia's money and Antonia's will provided the motive. It's all very well saying keep an open mind, what other motive could there be? Nothing but that damned will, that wasn't even like her. Robbery's out. His money wasn't touched. We looked through his things, nothing seemed to be missing.'

'No,' agreed the doctor, sighing. 'Everything was just as we might have expected to find it – nothing missing.'

There were so few of them left now. Five legatees, on equal terms, all with strong reasons for wishing Richard to die before he signed that hasty will of his; but she herself hadn't killed him, and neither had Laurence, and that left just three people, those three down there in the dining room.

Miranda? Was it even possible?

'Come to think of it,' said Trevor, in a voice suddenly sharpened by a note of surprise, 'shouldn't there have been something *un*expected among Richard's things?'

'What do you mean by that?'

'Whatever it was Antonia gave him, at the end. Something for Richard to remember her by! Have you forgotten? The last words of the great should always be written down at once. Whatever it was she gave him "to remember her by", he wouldn't wilingly have been parted from it.'

'Oh, that!' said the doctor with a sniff. 'We found that, surely. In his briefcase, that ivory miniature of her.'

'Oh, no!' said Trevor. 'Oh, dear, no! He's had that for years. Didn't you notice how worn it is? That's been round the world with him a couple of times.'

'Then what was it? And *where* was it? He'd never let it out of his care.'

Not an easy man to know, Trevor Mason. What was and what was not within his scope? He seemed to contain within himself curious contradictions. No one could be more considerate at times, no one could angle more viciously for his own ends when roused. Would he go as far as murder? How could you tell? Murderers were human creatures, too. And the doctor? He had fought like a demon to save Laurence, but did that necessarily prove that he hadn't also tried to kill him? Wouldn't it be the best possible way of covering himself, once he was called to the case? But on the other hand, if he'd wanted to finish his patient off wouldn't he have been able to do it very easily with the syringe, even before her eyes?

'But no, what's the good!' said the doctor vexedly. 'There's no getting away from that will and its provisions, it's nonsense to talk about robbery, and grub round for other motives. Such a motive for murder as that will couldn't exist by accident alongside a totally different motive. It's against the law of averages.'

The voices came and went in Susan's ears like a chorus to her thoughts, and some phrases she caught vividly, and some passed by her. This crashed abruptly large in her mind, like an entry of brass. Couldn't exist by accident, she repeated to herself, alongside a totally different— No, not by accident. But it could by design! To cover completely another motive and another murderer. Not by accident, by design. Except Antonia had made the will, and Antonia was dead, and could never have shaped her testament to bring about this monstrous mischief, living or dead. Besides, everything here was impromptu. Only the freakish weather had dropped them here, as vicious a piece of improvisation as – as a will composed to screen murder.

She stood up slowly, holding by the wall. She felt cold, but not with the cold of the night, from the heart outwards.

'No getting away from it,' said the doctor, still gnawing at his trouble. 'You can't ignore the evidence of your own eyes.'

'Ears,' said Trevor. 'Let's be accurate, at all costs.'

'Eh? What was that?'

'I said, ears. I didn't precisely see the provisions of the will, I heard them. Our friend Klostermann would call that hearsay evidence, I'm sure.'

He didn't know what he was saying, or that lightly ironic tone would have been frozen clean out of his voice. But she knew. The seed was late in dropping, but it rooted and grew and flowered like one of those speeded-up film sequences that produce monstrous prodigies of nature within the span of one minute. Everything was clear; truth was there to be seen. How little faith we really have even in the people we love, she thought, marvelling. Everyone said: 'It wasn't like her!' but no one ever said: '—therefore she never did it.' No, they turned round and said: 'She wasn't the person we thought her.' Even Richard. Even poor Richard.

She turned, and silently climbed the stairs, walking stiffly, with curious care, as though she trod unfamiliar ground that might shiver and gape under her feet.

Neil's door was not even locked. Neither was his

briefcase, when she found it in the wardrobe. It was as simple as that. She looked for the long envelope, and there it was, as soon as she snapped open the case. She drew out the thick folded form with its linen grain, and unfolded it under the bedside lamp, kneeling on the rug to read. It took her a long time, not only because of the legal phraseology, but also because she read with hypnotised slowness, taking every word into her consciousness with a deliberate effort, greedy for it and yet distrusting it. There was no hurry now. She had everything she needed, Laurence was safe. And Antonia was with her in the room. This was the very accent. This was the kind of person she was. No one would ever read this and say: 'But it wasn't like her.'

She had finished, and was folding the will again, when she heard the hand at the door, and felt the stirring of the air that went before the movements of a man's body. She whirled on her knees, clutching the papers to her breast, and stared with dilated eyes as Neil came in slowly, and slowly closed the door behind him.

He was looking at her without anger, with a terrible weary intelligence, as though he had been expecting her for a long time. She saw death in his face, and a bewildered, unassuageable sorrow; and in his hand, the last thing on earth she would ever have expected to see there, a small, shiny black gun.

CHAPTER XIV

As the hours that go, as the winds that blow,
So we twain will pass away.

Act 3

She gathered herself slowly, bracing her feet under her. She opened her mouth to scream, and knew that she could not; her throat was too dry, and the sheer effort was beyond her. It isn't easy to scream at will, when you have lived a life in which such antics never had a place.

'I shouldn't,' said Neil in a flat, tired voice. 'Because if you do I shall kill you. I shall have to, now that you know. You do see that, don't you?' He looked down for an instant at the hand that held the gun, and it seemed to astonish him as much as it astonished her. 'You'd never guess,' he said with a note of hopeless bewilderment in his voice, 'whose gun that was. I never handled one in my life until I took this from Richard's suitcase.'

'Along with the diamonds,' said Susan. The level tone she achieved was a surprise to her, it argued a sort of invulnerable continuity in her being, and she was encouraged; for a moment it had seemed to her that she had stopped existing, and could never resume on the old terms.

'No, those were in his briefcase. That's how I first

193

found out about them, when I fetched his case from the plane. I thought you'd have known that, since you know so much. Queer, isn't it, the things people do! I should have said Richard was the last man in the world to own a gun, but there it was. It seemed a kind of protection, so I took it. But I didn't really believe I should ever be using it.'

'You don't have to use it,' she said, her eyes still fixed unwaveringly on his face. 'I'm quiet. What are you going to do?'

'Run,' said the flat, sad voice. 'What else can I do now? And you're coming with me. I can't leave you here to start the hunt after me. I need time.' He passed a hand over his forehead, and something in the movement let her into the secret of the headache he was trying in vain to smooth away. 'Don't make any noise,' he said, 'or I shall kill you. I have to, you see, now that you know. Why did you have to find out? Everything was going so well, but you had to be the one who couldn't let me rest.'

Would he really fire? Was the gun even loaded? The hell of it is you can't tell by looking at it. But yes, he wouldn't neglect a thing like that. Even if he'd never touched one before, he'd make sure he knew how to use it. He'd been in extremity forty-eight hours now, he'd studied hard how to survive. She saw him brace his big shoulders and straighten his athletic back, and guessed at the weight he seemed to himself to be carrying; the world was not much more burdensome. Yes, he would fire if she made it necessary.

'Always you,' he said, 'always you between me and the light. Why? What did I ever do to you? I liked you! Get up, and put that will back in the briefcase.

No, stay facing me, I want to see your hands.'

They were trembling, but not as much as she had feared. Her nerves, unlike her mind, did not yet believe that she was within touch of death. She put the will back into the envelope, and into the briefcase, and closed the case upon it.

'Fasten your coat. Have you gloves? Take those woollen ones of mine.' Such care for the details of her comfort in the cold of the night, but the gun never wavered in his hand.

He reached behind him, and she heard the key turn in the lock; he was late with that precaution, but he was taking no chances now, the key went into his pocket before he moved sidewise to the wardrobe, and lifted out his coat. 'Don't!' he said, reading her mind. 'Don't make me. If you force me, I shall fire.'

It was a lame and humiliating business climbing so awkwardly into his coat, keeping his eyes on her, and the little black eye of the gun on her, too, except for snatched seconds while he slid either arm into its sleeve. But the touch of the ludicrous in his performance fell away before the hopeless, relentless grief in his face; and she remained very still, because she wanted to live. Laurence was safe, the shadow was slipping away from over him, whatever followed; with this knowledge in her, how detemined she was to live!

'Open the window!' Like hers, it opened on the balcony. Setting it wide, feeling the touch of the gun boring into her back, she thought, we shall have to pass the dining-room windows, someone will sense the movement and look out, we shall surely be seen. She dared not look round, but she knew he was close at her shoulder as she stepped through into the bitter wind and the thin, sudden snow. He had the briefcase under his arm, and he changed the gun to his left hand while he drew the long window closed after them; but she could not see his movements, and she walked before him with desperate care not to alarm or disconcert him. One involuntary convulsion of that tensed finger, and she would never tell anyone how true to form Antonia had run at the end of her life.

They went down the staircase, stepping cautiously on the frosty treads, she one pace ahead of him. They crossed the lighted windows, and the rising wind, howling desolately now, covered the sound of their steps, and the thin, driving snow beating diagonally across the glass made them only a vaguely moving shadow in the darkness. No one came to the window to peer after them, no one called out.

'Go on,' said Neil. She felt his breath gusty against her temple. 'Through the village to the track. Go faster.'

She tried; she was afraid not to try, and yet she was afraid of the thin coating of new snow on the hard ice of the road, afraid of trying to hurry where she could not even see the ground properly for the slashing fall and the shifting darkness. Glass would have been safe walking by comparison. The small, frozen flakes stung her cheeks and lips and melted in her lashes, blinding her. She hugged the edge of the beaten track, where she could hope to wedge her feet into untrodden places, but through two days other people had been making use of the same meagre rims, and there was hardly a square inch left that was not polished ice. Slipping and recovering, balancing as best she could, she was thrust forward into the wind.

'You won't get through,' she cried, straining her voice against the whining storm. 'It's getting worse.'

'I shall,' he said.

'They'll be looking for you.'

'Oh, no, not yet. He's finished with me. Randall will keep him happy for a long time, and then there are the others.'

'But in the end they'll go to wake me.'

'Not for some time yet. Long enough.'

She was horribly afraid he might be right. The village was so small, the way through it so short, already they were half-way to that distant rim where the houses fell behind, and the ground slipped away into a gully among the rocks, easily blocked by heavy snows. And people went to bed at a respectable hour, no one was stirring in all that whitened darkness. Even Fritzi was sleeping long ago after his errand.

Then she remembered McHugh, and hope sprang up in her like a sudden recovering flame in a fire which had seemed quite dead. One man at least was awake in this extinguished village. Somewhere between here and that left turning between the houses they must surely meet him. He must have had her message long ago, now he could repay her for the warning. But why hadn't he made his appearance already? The distance was not so great, and he must surely have taken the hint at once.

Thinly between the wails of the strengthening wind she heard what seemed for a moment like a human voice crying; but the wind on a squally night plays queer tricks. The fist in her back jabbed home the gun warningly; Neil had heard it, too. It came from somewhere ahead of them, if they could have drawn aside the whirling snow like a veil to see a few

197

yards before their faces. Something dark lay in the
snow by the side of the tracks, and heaved and
moved awkwardly towards them. Two outstretched
arms flattened laborious hands along the ice and
heaved again. They were quite near the narrow
turning to Frau Agathe's house now, it must be only
a few yards beyond that smudge in the snow. Susan
cleared her eyes with her hand, and peered forward,
and knew she was looking at McHugh.

She thought first, with a rush of concern for him:
'He's hurt!' and then for herself, even more bitterly:
'He's disabled!' The last waking man, and he had to
turn careless in his haste, and bring himself down
on the ice with broken bones, like a brittle old lady
going out to post a letter on a frosty night. He, who
was so confident of his body, and so cocksure in his
superb control of it, he had to be brought down from
his high horse on this night of all nights, when his
fall could do the maximum damage to everyone
round him.

'Go on!' said Neil hoarsely in her ear, and the gun
ground into her back. 'Don't stop. Don't speak.'

To be silent will be to speak, she thought, if he's
conscious. 'He's hurt,' she said. 'Let me stay and help
him. You'll go faster without me.'

'Go on, damn you, and shut up. Pass him.' The
weight of despair in the voice was such that she
thought it should have been he who was broken to
the ground under it. From between the outstretched
arms already filmed with new flakes McHugh lifted
his head, and the pallor of his face was turned to
them with a great moaning sigh of relief. In a moment
she would be able to bend and touch him; only, of
course, she could not. Suddenly that hurt even more

than her own fear. Tears contorted the vague images before her into a dazzle of black and white.

'Let me help him! You can't leave him. You can manage to kill people, in a distant sort of way, I can understand that, but you can't just walk past an injured man and leave him to freeze to death.'

'Go on!' he whispered in a strangled voice. 'And shut your mouth, or I'll kill you! Whatever happens afterwards, I'll kill you!'

She cast one glance at him, the first she had ventured since they set out, and saw his face for a moment twisted into a theatre mask of appalling grief; and it seemed to her that this moment marked for him the formal and irrevocable sentence of his banishment from the world in which he had moved blamelessly all his life until now. He had left it without knowing what he did, but now in every step it forced him away, and in every image that marked the stages of his going he saw reflected everything he had lost.

McHugh croaked: 'Everard, thank God! I thought I'd never—'

They passed by him, hurrying, stumbling, their faces set and strained, with eyes fixed blindly ahead. In awful amazement he, too, fell silent, unable to understand or believe, as though two dead people had walked past him in the white of noon. The moment bound them all three in a constricting circle of silence and dread. Only when they were by him, and the indifferent snow slashed between, did he heave himself up on his elbows and begin to shout after them frantically: 'Everard, what the hell are you doing? Come back here! Give me a hand, damn you, my leg's broken—'

The whining wind soon took the words and tore them to shreds, and even the sound might have been no more than the fretted gale tangled in the palings of the fence. They were soon out of earshot. It was doubtful if his cries would be heard from any of the houses, with that wind blowing.

The last fence fell behind. The path declined, zig-zagging with the gully as meticulously as a brook, and across the last open ground the increasing snow danced and whirled dizzily. They groped their way down to where the rocks began, and halted to draw breath and clear their eyes in the shelter of the first jagged face.

'You could still go back,' she said. Even if he did kill her she could not help saying it. But perhaps it wasn't even true; perhaps the only terms on which he could go back were such as to make it, for him, an impossibility. 'You could still turn back and help him.'

'Go on,' he said, and pushed her forward down the tortuous track between the rocks. Already the wind had driven in snow knee-deep, smoothing out all the tracks Klostermann and his fellows had left on their way up. By morning the road might very well be sealed again. Where freaks of air and rock formation gave the gale play Susan floundered up to the waist, and felt her way by the boulders, for her eyes were useless. Out of the valley below snow boiled upwards like mist, carried on rising eddies.

She paused for a moment, panting, her back braced against the rock. 'You can't kill everyone,' she cried. 'Him, me, everyone who crosses your path. We didn't speak to him. What then? Nothing could have shouted louder. They'll know. It was inevitable from the time I got to know. It was always inevitable, really.' She was no longer shouting, because he had been glad to halt, too, and was leaning breast to breast with her in the lee of the rocks, in a little island of quietness hedged in from the gale. He was no less distressed than she was. She could hear the breath sobbing between his lips. 'Turn back now,' she said.

'I wish to God I could,' he said quite gently, with terrifying resignation. 'Don't you think I'd unwind all this and be my old self again if I could? You can't go back. Once you kill somebody there's no going back.' His face was very close. What faint light there was seemed to gather into the great aching expanse of his forehead beneath the wet red-brown hair whitened over with snow. He still had the briefcase clutched under his left arm, and his right hand was deep in the pocket of his coat, but she knew that it was still clenched on the gun. 'It was so easy,' he said with a kind of tired wonder. 'I didn't even have to touch him, I didn't feel soiled at all. Only after that there was no going back, and no standing still. Events kept pushing me forward. *You* kept pushing me forward. Forcing my hand. You're still doing it. Making me kill you. I never wanted to kill you.'

She had known all along, in her heart, that that was his intention. However his disappearance and hers might cast suspicion on him, it could not of itself convict him of murder, even of hers. No one but she could ever tell them the truth about Antonia's will and the Treplenburg-Feldstein diamonds. If she never reappeared living, no one else would ever know. That could at least confuse the issue, and this delay might, with luck, afford him enough time to get clear away, especially if the blizzard sealed this road again before morning. But she would not survive to slow him up much longer, she perfectly understood that. Time was what he could least afford.

'Even with me dead events will still keep pushing you on,' she said, 'the only way to stop them is to turn and face them.'

The deep, sighing breaths – they laboured rather with the weight upon his heart than with any load of physical weariness – gathered strength slowly to answer: 'I've thought of that.'

It all came out quite simply, as if it eased him to share the intolerable load with her. 'When you're gone I'm going back. I shall tell them I looked in on you to see if you were awake, and found you'd gone – run away. Because you were lying in trying to give Laurence an alibi, and now that the police had arrived you'd lost your nerve. You'd be an accessory after the fact, you see. So you ran away. I went out to look for you and bring you back, but I couldn't find you. But we shall find you, tomorrow, when it's light. You'll have slipped from the path below here, where the ground falls away on one side. It's quite a drop – and the snow will do the rest. Nobody else has seen the will, you know, so I shall easily be believed. I'll destroy the will if I have to – I can account for that somehow. Oh, yes, I shall be believed.'

There was no complacency in that flat, sorrowful voice, and no triumph; she thought she could have borne it better if there had been. To be killed was enough, surely, but to be killed without even removing the shadow of death from Laurence was such aggravated cruelty that she felt in herself suddenly what this man had never felt, the honest, burning desire to kill, the impulse of absolute anger, almost too great to be contained, far too great to be expressed in any senseless, pointless words or motions of rage. She fought as she could, hacking mercilessly at the ground under his feet.

'So I ran away – without my money, without my passport? Who's going to believe that of me?'

'They'll believe it,' he said, his chest heaving. 'I'll make it plausible. When people panic they do crazy things.'

'And who's ever seen me panic? Have you? Am I panicking now? Those people know me better than you do, they won't swallow that tale. And besides,' she said, smiling up at him fiercely, and shoving from her forehead the wet dark tendrils of her hair, 'in that case you should have killed McHugh, shouldn't you? Nobody has to convince him of anything. He *knows*! No good telling *him* I ran away and you followed to try and bring me back – *he saw* us go!'

'He won't be sharing what he knows with anyone else,' panted Neil, wrenching his face aside from the glare of her vengeful eyes. 'The snow and frost will take care of him.'

'He's indoors by now, and you know it. He'll shout until someone does come and help him – someone who hasn't kicked himself out of the human race—'

'Nobody'll hear him! The wind will drown his voice—'

'Then he'll crawl to one of the houses. And don't forget they'll be looking for me by now. When they don't find me in the house they'll search outside. They'll find McHugh. And he'll tell them how you and I left the village. You see,' she said, spitting the words in his face, 'there'll always be somebody else you have to kill, more and more and more of them. They multiply. You might as well give up now. There's no end to it.'

And indeed he saw no end, look as far ahead as he would, never any end to the killing; and always the revulsion from it, that mounted in horror every time, as though death itself could be eternally reproduced upon his own flesh. He bowed forward over her with a sob, and leaned his forehead against the rock above her shoulder, and cried brokenly in his desolation; but he did not relax his fingers from the butt of the gun that bruised her side.

CHAPTER XV

Fear naught, whatever may befall!
To save you now must be my one endeavour,
And yet I know not how.

Act 2

Laurence had been left alone in his room until he was damned if he was going to stand it any longer. A dozen times since that bad break at midday he had enquired anxiously whether Susan had reappeared, and been told with varying degrees of exasperation that she had not, and that when she did he would be informed. But it had gone on so long that he no longer quite trusted even Dr Randall. And now it seemed the working-party from the lower village had cut their way through, and with them Frau Agathe's policeman, and the whole case was being taken to pieces and put together again in one more hopeless inquest; but no one came near him. Somewhere down there arguments were being piled up against him in his absence, which was patently unfair, if he had had a thought to spare for it; but his real grievance was that they were still keeping him from Susan.

He had slept again, and eaten heartily, and he felt encouragingly normal; so as there was no one to order him back to bed he got up and tried his legs

about the bedroom, and found them only slightly
shaky under him. He was perfectly all right, apart
from a slightly hollow and queasy feeling which had
nothing to do with hunger, a decided stiffness and
soreness of all his muscles, as though he had been
beaten all over, and a sharp local discomfort,
reminiscent of his unco-operative schooldays, when
he sat down too briskly on a wooden chair to pull
on his socks. He dressed with the slightly clumsy
movements of convalescence, and while he was
combing his hair roughly into order he heard, faintly
crossing the end of his isolated corridor, light
footsteps which he recognised as belonging to Liesl.

He threw down his comb to pummel the door with
both fists, and then changed his mind just in time.
If he did that she'd never risk opening the door. He
was supposed to be in bed, and still so nearly an
invalid as to be no threat to any girl's peace of mind.
He called instead. A weak and plaintive appeal
would have fetched her like a bird, but for the fact
that it would never have reached her ears. He com-
promised, calling her name just loudly enough to
make himself heard, and just pathetically enough to
incline her to listen.

The footsteps halted; she came hesitantly to his
door. 'Do you want something, Mr Quayne?'

'I'm sorry to trouble you, but I'm not allowed to
get up and get it for myself – I'd like a book out of
my suitcase, if you'd give it to me, please. I want to
stay awake, they'll want me presently. And there's
nobody to talk to. I must do *something*.' He was
almost ashamed of the facility with which he
achieved that appealing note; his shoulders all the
while flattened against the wall behind the door,

and his voice pitched in such a subdued key that she should not detect his nearness to her.

She had her keys still in her pocket, he heard the jingle of the bunch as she separated the one she wanted. 'Of course, Mr Quayne, I will get it.' The door opened confidingly, she stepped into the room and took two or three trusting paces before she realised the bed was empty. At the same moment the door was taken firmly from her hand; he was not going to have her darting out again and slamming it in his face.

She gave a soft, startled cry of reproach. 'Oh, Mr Quayne, you must not – you should not—'

'Oh, don't be an ass!' he said. 'I won't hurt you, and I'm not doing any harm, but I'm sick of being in quarantine up here like a case of bubonic plague. I've as much right to be down there keeping an eye on my own interests as any of the rest of them. And besides, I want to see Susan. Where is she?'

'But you are ill,' she said, spreading her pretty arms gently as if she would shoo him back into his bed like a chicken into its pen. 'You should not be up, you know it well, the doctor said—'

'I feel perfectly well, and I want to talk to Susan. Is she down there with them? Where? In the dining room?'

'No, she is still in her room, I was just going to wake her. But, please, I cannot let you—'

'Dear Liesl, you can't stop me.' He was out in the corridor and heading for Susan's door. Liesl trotted agitatedly at his heels, fluttering like a ruffled bird. 'Nobody's going to blame you, and anyhow, I'll go down and give myself up like a lamb, once I've talked to Susan. We'll go down together, I promise you.'

He took her gently by the shoulders, and stood her in front of the closed door of Susan's room. 'Now you go in and say a good word for me, like a good girl. Tell her I'm outside putting ashes on my head, and ask her not to hit me when I'm down.'

Never in his life had he looked or felt less down than now. He didn't know why, but he carried in him a hopefulness on which nothing could make a mark; not death, nor injustice, nor suspicion, nor ill-feeling between man and man. He thought of Susan lying asleep not three yards away from him, on the other side of that door, and everything was well with him.

Liesl rapped softly, and got no answer. She turned the handle and went in. He didn't try to follow her, he waited dutifully in the middle of the corridor, his heart beating a little more rapidly, with an optimism nothing could subdue.

'It is strange,' said Liesl, 'she is not here. She must have gone down only this moment, when you called me to your room.'

He went in then, and snapped on the light. The room was empty, the bed empty, the covers turned back as she had left them. He was not disturbed, not yet. He turned and ran down the stairs and into the dining room, where Miranda and Dr Randall waited, but Susan was not there either. His mother jumped up and embraced him with the unusual warmth generated by her own weariness and anxiety. He hugged her abstractedly, his eyes roving the room quickly over her shoulder, and the eager gleam faded out of them before the first shadow of uneasiness.

'Laurence, dear, has he let you out, then? Does he realise—?'

'Where's Susan?' asked Laurence directly. 'Have you seen her?'

'She's still in her room,' said the doctor. 'Liesl has gone up to wake her. I hadn't forgotten about you. And when did I tell you you could get up?'

'I know about Liesl, I've just left her upstairs. But Susan isn't there. We thought she must have come down.'

'No,' said the two voices at once. Miranda went on somewhat acidly: 'You may be sure she's somewhere about the house, quite safe and well. Why should you question her movements? It's high time you considered your own position. I told that young man: "My son is entirely innocent, and you have no right to cast doubts—" '

'I'm sure you did, Mother,' said Laurence automatically, and took his arms from her abruptly and plunged back through the hall. The floor still had a tendency to go slightly soft under his feet, but it was steadying. Anxiety over Susan froze everything into sharp definition again, even the yielding bones of his legs. He flung open the door of the little office, and erupted into the room like a blast of cold outer air.

'We've lost Susan,' he said, casting the statement accusingly into Klostermann's astonished face, and remembered with exasperation that if he wanted to be understood he should have said it in German, as well as somewhat elaborating the bald fact. Either exercise was beyond him. He turned instead upon Trevor Mason, who apparently could converse with his questioner well enough without an interpreter.

'She isn't in her room, and nobody's seen her down here, and I'm worried. We ought to look for her. I don't like mislaying Susan, not at this hour of night, and while we've still got a murderer around.'

Miranda pulled irately at his arm. 'You're being very silly. In all probability she's in the bathroom, since apparently she's just got out of bed—'

'She hasn't just got out of bed. The bed's cold. And she isn't in the bathroom. I just came past it on my way down, and the door's ajar and the light's off. Tell him, Trevor! We've got to find her.'

Trevor interpreted inexpertly but effectively. Dr Randall, pressing in at Miranda's shoulder, suggested: 'Perhaps she took her tray back to the kitchen,' and trotted away to see before Laurence could save him the trouble; for her tray was still untouched in her bedroom. Klostermann got up from behind the table, a thick-set quiet man of thirty or so, with a weathered, long-sighted mountaineer's face. His intelligent and lively eyes flashed from face to face, settled longest on Laurence. Still studying him, he asked brief questions of Trevor, and gathering up the array of papers ranged neatly over the table, swept them back into the safe.

The doctor returned from the kitchen with Franz on his heels, and Liesl, running down the stairs, said in a voice high-pitched with uneasiness: 'Her coat is gone. And her boots, those pretty snow boots, they are gone, too. I do not understand. Where could she go at this hour?'

Klostermann cast one quick glance round them all. Frau Mehlert was in bed and asleep, but by now this sudden tension had drawn together all the rest of the household. All but one.

'*Wo ist* Herr Everard?' he asked.

No one knew. No one had seen him since he emerged from the office and went upstairs. Franz ran to look for him in his room. He was not there, and his bed had not been disturbed. The wardrobe door swung open, a hanger had fallen to the floor. The window on the balcony was closed, but an edge of the long curtain was caught in it; as soon as the inner window was opened to release it a flurry of new snow fell into the room with it and blew in feathery petals across the rug.

Then everyone in the house was caught up into the hunt. They reached for coats and anoraks and sweaters, and the trail-breakers came pouring out from the bar steamy and warm after their coffee and rum. The driving wind met them on the doorstep. The snow was drifting high along the cleared track, piled in a great smooth wave wherever the sheltering bulk of the houses and fences parted. The searchers covered their faces and headed southwards, downhill through the village; there was no other way to go, if the lost ones had hoped to reach any other habitable place in this world.

Laurence, in a gigantic borrowed sweater pulled hurriedly over his own, was first into the slashing wind, head-down, running recklessly in his hopelessly inadequate shoes, stumbling, wading through drifts, slipping and falling and fending himself off and running on again. He did not know what had happened, but he knew that there was about it something so wrong and false that it must be undone. Susan was gone, Neil was gone. What did it mean to those others, spreading out now behind him to comb through the village and the valley? That they had some reason in common for vanishing, some guilty reason which they feared to be in danger of discovery? That they had run together? He did not

211

believe it. He knew her, however he had tried to deny his knowledge because she had hurt him so cruelly. It was with him, not with Neil, she had spent that strange Christmas Eve. She had nothing to run from, even if she had been the kind to run away. He floundered through the snow and the whirling darkness, not thinking at all, only feeling; and what he felt, so passionately that there was no room in him for anything else, was terror for her, and love for her, and the piercing necessity for finding her. Everything else, everything in the world, could wait for that.

He halted in the middle of the track, and cupped his hands round his mouth to shout ahead into the wind. A faint cry, tossed among the gusts like wandering snow, answered him. He groped towards it, fearful and hopeful, though his senses told him it was not her voice, and he was even afraid that he had made a mistake in calling out at all. Blinded with snow, he blundered into the fence on the left side of the road, and clawing his way along it, fell over something that heaved feebly and darkly out of the whiteness. His outstretched hands found a sleeve, and a shoulder that jerked upwards, breaking the crust of snow as a mole breaks ground.

He got his arm under a heavy head and raised it, clearing away snow from the clogged eyes and gasping mouth with his mittened hand.

'McHugh! My God, what happened to you? You're hurt?'

'Leg,' shivered the blue lips, weakly spitting out snow. 'Broken. Too big a hurry – bloody silly trick–'

'Hold up, we'll soon get you home. They're close behind me.' Laurence turned his chin on his shoulder, and sent a great bellow back along the road towards the search parties.

'Shouted – nobody heard me— Couldn't reach – blasted latch of – gate.' McHugh heaved himself higher against the supporting shoulder, and panted: 'All right now, you go on!'

Laurence shouted again, and was answered. Dark figures loomed out of the murk, wading towards them. 'Here!' he yelled. 'It's McHugh. He's had a fall. He's hurt!'

'You go on!' McHugh swallowed the trickles of snow that crumbled into his mouth. 'They went past me – that way. Something's wrong—'

'Went past you? They – who? Was it Susan? Susan and Everard? Not together?'

'Yes – down that way—'

'They walked past you?' shouted Laurence frantically. 'What, and left you lying here like this? *Susan?*'

'No choice,' mumbled the cold mouth, labouring painfully. 'He made her – never spoke a word, but he made her. Go on after them – looked like death – both of 'em—'

Already braced to run, Laurence looked back in agonised hesitation. Klostermann was ploughing manfully through the last yards of the drift, the doctor close beside him, and after them came three of the men from Bad Schwandegg.

'Run!' insisted McHugh, feebly pushing him. 'Leave me, I'm fine. I'll tell them.'

Laurence scrambled to his feet and ran. As he disappeared on the downward road Dr Randall was on his knees in the drift beside the casualty, feeling his way gingerly down the distorted left leg, and Franz and two of the others were taking the nearest yard gate off its hinges. Laurence did not look back. He was at the rim of the village, where the open ground began, when they carefully lifted the injured man on to their improvised stretcher, and shed a couple of coats to cushion his head and cover him.

It was their efficiency that shut his mouth too soon, for he had not succeeded in fumbling out a coherent statement and making them pay attention to it before they raised him, and gentle and expert though they were, he fainted under their hands. By the time he came round they had him in the warmth of the inn kitchen, and it took him several minutes more to remember what it was he had to do, and to make a good job of it. Then they left him to the doctor's care and set off again in haste into the night, calling the other searchers as they went; but Laurence was far ahead, and struggling downhill among the rocks.

Enough snow had fallen to smooth out all outlines. He waded as in water, unable to judge at any thrust forward how far he might have to fall. To be cautious was to be slow, and time was the one thing he could not afford, or so he thought until he stepped astray in his blindness and crashed painfully into a narrow crevice between boulders. He dragged himself clear again, shaken but intact, thinking of McHugh stranded with a fractured leg in the very village street, and for a little while he went less recklessly, for if he disabled himself what would happen to Susan?

But for every niggling devil in his mind urging him to be careful, ten were screaming at him to be quick, and he did not slacken his pace for long. Down the tortuous zigzags between the rock faces he crashed in a series of ricochets, fending himself off with spread hands at the turns, sliding in flurries of dislodged snow, falling breast-deep into drifts in exposed places, once slithering sidewise from the track into a hole which engulfed him in soft snow above his head, and crawling out again with half the skin of one cheek scored into ribbons by the rock. When he had to slow to a crawl he could feel himself shaking crazily, with a violence that alarmed him rather for his effectiveness than for his own safety; but when he was able to move at speed he had no time to be aware of the shortcomings of his body, and it served him well because it had to.

He saw nothing of anyone or anything moving ahead. The ground here was too broken and complex, even if the driving snow had not reduced visibility to a few yards. But presently the fall seemed to him to be slackening, or the high bulk of the mountain wall on the right made this particular stretch calmer, and the rocky gully opened out for a while into a narrow valley where it was possible to move more freely. He launched himself rashly down these gentler slopes, using his long legs like a scree runner, and reckless of the irregularities of surface that might lie beneath the uniform whiteness.

There was another brief passage among rocks, a series of blind corners where you might come face to face with an enemy round any boulder, or overtake him and have him in your arms before you were aware; and then an open shoulder of the mountain, calm as a meadow. There he suddenly saw the miracle of their tracks before him, an uneven furrow ploughed across a white field. They were so close that the wind had had no time to silt up their pathway, or even file smooth its jagged edges. He saw where the single furrow split into two for a few paces, and his heart leaped, and he pushed forward with fresh vigour.

The meadow terminated in a raised crest and a short, undulating plunge to where a steep and broken slope began; and here the path continued on its way to the valley by a narrow shelf, the bulk of the mountain on the right hand and the uncomfortable drop on the left. Laurence climbed panting over the crest, and looking down, saw his quarry below him. There was no doubt of it. The thin fall between them and him was no more than a fluttering veil now, though below the broken descent mist and snow together boiled up out of the valley and hid the rest of the world from him.

Two small dark figures, close together, approached the beginning of the traverse. The path beyond was only a faint white diagonal along the mottled slope, so masked with snow that it hardly broke the angle of descent.

Laurence ran slithering down the deeply scored track they had left, and they vanished from his sight. One more rise, and he emerged suddenly so close to them that he dropped into the snow in terror that he might have been seen. Less than thirty steep, descending yards away from him they pushed reeling forward, their clogged movements heavy with exhaustion. They were very close to the edge now. He saw Susan turn her head, and caught a glimpse of the pallor of her face. He thought he heard the blown threads of their voices. Very clearly he saw how Neil's right arm propelled her forward, nearer and nearer to where she must step on to the shelf

216

path. It was sheer madness to attempt that traverse in darkness. She hung back, afraid of it, but he still pushed her forward. She crumpled under his hand suddenly, and went down into the snow, and lay huddled with her head bowed into her arms. Neil took her by the sleeve and tried to jerk her to her feet, and for want of the strength to lift her, suddenly kicked at her with all the force he had left.

Laurence launched himself downhill with a yell of rage that cut through the wind and brought them both round to stare up at him wildly. He caught one glimpse of Susan's face, great desperate eyes that flared suddenly into recognition and joy, and a panting mouth that shrieked at him: 'Look out, he has a gun!'

He was aware, even as he crashed down on them like a flung stone, of the shock of astonishment. He had not reckoned with guns, they were things he had never encountered in his life until now.

It was his recklessness that saved him. He came down in a rolling fall, sweeping a bow wave of snow with him, and Neil's bullet ploughed harmlessly into the ground behind him; if he had been still on his feet it would have found its mark somewhere high in his body. His impetus carried him right to Neil's feet, and swept them both a yard nearer to the edge of the drop. He rolled to his knees and clutched Neil about the thighs, trying to bring him down. Neil braced himself back to resist the pull, and clubbed viciously at the uplifted face with fist and gun together.

Dimly, through the explosions of pain, Laurence heard Susan scream. He ground his head hard into Neil's body to shelter from the senseless, frenzied blows, and shifted his grip lower, wrenching at the stiffened knees. It had better be short, he was in no case to keep this up for long, even if he had ever had any skill in fighting. He heaved with all his strength, and down came Neil in the snow with him, and they rolled together, wrestling frantically for the gun. Laurence realised then why Neil had used only one hand, his gun hand, to batter off the assault. He had been clutching something tightly to his body under his left arm, and with his fall it had been flung out of his hold. It dropped into the snow, and Susan threw herself full-length along the trampled ground and snatched it away.

Neil had felt it go from him as sharply as he might have felt a wound. He stretched out his hand vainly after it, turning his head for one instant with a lamentable cry. Laurence lunged for the gun, gripping the tensed wrist and straining to force the fingers open, but the moment of distraction was already past. His attention torn back perforce, Neil shoved him off frantically to the full length of his left arm as they rolled on the ground, and drawing up a knee between them, drove his foot hard into his opponent's groin. Laurence's grip broke. He curled upon himself, groaning, doubled over the pain, and came sickly to his knees; and Neil, scrambling out of reach, lurched to his feet and levelled the gun for the kill.

Susan shrieked: 'Neil!' on so terrible a note of frenzy that he wavered, half-turning towards her. She had stumbled to the edge of the drop, the brief-case clutched in her hands. She knew what she had to do; suddenly it was quite clear and very simple. She swung the briefcase by its handle and flung it out over the void. It fell, twisting and turning slowly, and the boiling mist swallowed it. Far down the steep, invisible slope they heard it fall and rebound; and then there was nothing but the rustle of snow silting downwards from the edge of the scar.

Neil uttered an incredible, heart-rending sound, a wail of inhuman despair; it was as if the wind had risen and wrung suddenly at a harp of naked trees. He turned from Laurence and sprang to the edge of the slope, peering down hopelessly into the shifting mists, weaving like a frantic animal driven by one fear and halted by another. The breath sobbed through his lips in little whimpering cries of frustration and desire. He put a foot over the edge, drew back afraid, flung himself on his knees in the snow and let himself down backwards into the void, scrambling and slipping desperately after the prize for which he had thrown away his world. He could not be parted from it, it was all he had left.

The gun was torn from his hand, and he let it go, spreading his fingers like claws to check his rolling descent. Broken faces of snow slid from the tattered slope and ran with him, half-burying him. Once Susan saw him raise his face and look up at her, and then the mist and the snow and the dizzy, falling distances took him and swallowed him up, and there was only the continuous rustling sound, diminuendo, smaller at last than the wind's moaning.

She covered her eyes, and began to sob tearlessly. Not for him, not for herself, not even for Laurence, only for the terrible waste of it all. For one moment he had looked like the old Neil again, peering forward in incredulous astonishment at the new.

Laurence staggered to his feet, limped the few

yards to her, and put his arms round her without a word. There was no physical assurance about Laurence, he touched her even now with the old constraint, until she turned and buried her face desperately in his shoulder, and locking her arms about his body, clung to him as though she wanted to grow into him and be lost. Then he stopped trembling, and tightened his hold on her for the first time as though he felt he might really have rights in her.

'Come away,' he said breathlessly into her ear. 'Come along, I'm taking you back.'

'He'll die,' she said, reassuring herself. It was better that he should. What was there left for him now? The night and the snow would take care of him, even if the broken face of the mountain refused him a death.

Laurence hadn't understood. That was like him, too; she hoped he never would. 'We'll come back for him,' he promised gently. 'We'll try to find him, don't worry, we won't leave him to freeze. But first I'm taking you home.'

She lifted her face out of his shoulder and drew his head down to her, holding him fast against her cheek until his warmth passed into her and calmed her. 'Oh, Laurence!' she said in a great sigh, and ceased to shudder. 'Oh, Laurence! Oh, Laurence!'

They left the gun where it lay, only a few feet below the path, and struggled up the rolling meadow together, he helping her forward tenderly in his arm as long as they could move abreast. He was shaking with the weakness left over from his brush with death twenty-four hours ago, scratched and bruised from his hasty pursuit of her, wet and chilled through, and limping from Neil's kick; and he had forgotten to feel any of these handicaps, because she was leaning on him. It wasn't difficult to see how his mother had been able to live on him emotionally, as well as economically, all these years. He was even somewhat sick and sore with himself for not being more adequate, she could feel it in the pressure of his arm, and in his hard, controlled breathing. He would have liked to be able to loose a dramatic punch and lay his opponent senseless. Everybody always wants to be what he isn't. But there was nothing about him, from the crown of his battered, straw-coloured head to the soles of his sodden shoes, that Susan wanted changed.

The snow had almost stopped, which eased their distress on the long climb back. It took them a weary time to reach the second defile among the rocks; but there they heard the welcome sound of men descending, and were met by Klostermann and his companions, coming down in haste to look for them.

CHAPTER XVI

Who was it called for help? Who broke the peace?

Act 3

The warmth of the inn and the hysteria of their welcome, Miranda's tears and embraces, Trevor's frantic questions, the flurry of excitement and concern, swept over them like a tidal wave, and almost overwhelmed them in the heaviness and nausea of exhaustion. They allowed themselves to be engulfed, subsiding into a daze through which fleeting voices flashed like lightning. 'Are you all right?' 'Where's Everard?' 'What happened?' 'Tried to kill you! – what, *Neil Everard*?' 'Gun? What gun? Nobody here has a gun.'

They tried to answer, but speech was too much effort. Franz came to their rescue with hot, strong drinks that went down like fire, and the doctor, coming in haste from McHugh's bedside to confirm that the truants were safely home, had them both hustled upstairs instantly, stripped of their sodden clothes by hands less cold and clumsy than their own, and chased into hot baths. By the time they emerged in dry clothes the shock and sickness were gone, and when he tried to persuade them to go sensibly to bed they resisted his authority strenuously.

'I couldn't rest,' said Susan, 'not until the men come back, not until we know what's happened. Laurence wanted to turn back with them, to show them the place, but Herr Klostermann wouldn't let him. I don't want to be alone yet. I'd rather be with the others. And besides, I'm *hungry*!'

'Well, then, if you must go down,' said the doctor resignedly, 'you might just look in and have a word with McHugh before you go. He's been asking for you. I told him you were all right, but he'll be happier if he sees for himself. Go and talk to him, then maybe he'll sleep.'

She went in quietly, but McHugh's head turned at once as the door opened, and his bright, wide-awake eyes saluted her with a somewhat distorted smile. The bedside lamp was turned so that it would not shine on his face, and over his legs they had erected an improvised cage that bulged the feather quilt like an aeroplane hangar under snow.

'You *are* intact,' he said. 'That's good. I wasn't much help to you, I'm afraid. Sorry!'

'Neither was I to you.' She came hesitantly to the bedside. 'I'm terribly sorry about your leg.'

'You can sit on the edge of the bed, my cage is stable enough. Know what they built it out of? Barrel hoops. I call that appropriate.' He smiled up at her and was silent for a moment. 'I just wanted to have a look at you, and make sure they were telling me the truth. I shouldn't have liked it if anything had happened to you, I shouldn't have liked it at all. And I also want to say thank you.'

'It wasn't for you I did it,' she said, not unkindly, only by way of being absolutely honest about it. 'I just didn't see why it should be blown up into a tragedy. Nobody deserved that.'

'Not even me?' She expected him to ask how she had known, but he did not. He had always a way of sticking to essentials. 'Well, I've got my wages. I don't know if the doctor told you – he didn't tell me, for that matter, but I know – I've made a pretty bad mess of this fracture. With what I've done to myself this time, I shall probably be grounded for good. There are several able-bodied kids waiting to step into my shoes. It looks as if my wife will be seeing a good deal more of me from now on.'

She looked at him doubtfully, suspicious of the placid tone, but the black eyes were equally calm. 'Don't be sorry,' he said. 'I asked for it, I'm not complaining. Only one thing, though – you'll understand I couldn't ask anyone else. Was there plenty of snow? I can't remember too well, and I must have left a pretty noticeable trail. It would be a pity to waste it all now.'

She understood. 'Plenty of snow, don't worry. Nobody's ever going to follow your trail. They found you in the main street, where anyone has a right to be.'

'Thank God!' he sighed, and closed his eyes for a moment.

'How far did you drag yourself?' she asked, with a suspicion of the truth in her already.

'Right from her gate. I'd barely shut it behind me when I crashed. Me, the master equilibrist – tight-ropes and thin ice my specialities!'

'And she didn't come and help you?' said Susan incredulously.

'She didn't know.'

'You didn't call for help?'

'There? On her doorstep? No, I reckoned I could get to the road without passing out. I owed her that. Don't look at me like that,' he said, smiling up at her ruefully. 'You're undoing all the good effect of what the beaks call a "short, sharp lesson". The one bad thing nobody can say about me, Susan, is that I whine about carrying the can.'

'No,' she agreed gently, 'that's one thing I'll never say about you.'

'Then do me one more favour. Tomorrow, when Agathe comes, tell her I'm all right, and not to worry, and that I shan't be bothering her again. In a few days they'll be able to get me out of here to hospital, and until then I shall be tucked well out of her way. Say I wish her all the best.'

'I'll tell her,' said Susan.

She had almost reached the door on her way out when he added: 'And give her my love.' She looked back doubtfully; the grin he flashed her still had a reserve of dangerous impudence. 'My *respectful* love, of course!'

Susan went down the stairs very thoughtfully. Never again would she be quite so arrogantly certain of her snap judgments of people; McHugh was not the only one who had been treated to a lesson in Oberschwandegg, they were none of them going back unchanged.

They were in the dining room, waiting for her with fresh supplies of hot coffee, and the tray of food she had left untouched in her room. The bruises were beginning to darken and swell on Laurence's forehead and cheek, and his eyes were feverishly bright after all the spirits Franz had poured into him. They sat opposite each other, flushed now instead of pale, looking curiously alike in spite of all their differences of colouring and feature, each with a scratched left cheek, each with damp hair curling steamily in the warmth of the room, each a little drunk with rum and brandy and the newly appreciated intoxication of being alive. Between them they told the story of the night's adventure, very lamely. Neither of them wanted to remember too closely or too clearly as yet.

'Everard!' said the doctor in a long, incredulous breath. 'And there's no doubt of it? He admitted it?'

'He told me himself. He said: "It was so easy, I didn't even have to touch him. Only after that there was no turning back." ' She heard again the aching, hopeless voice, and shivered over her coffee.

'You had a start on the rest of us,' said Trevor, 'knowing as you did, that Laurence was out of it. But I still don't see how you arrived at Everard. Everard, of all people! Here were all five of us with a solid motive, and Everard with none at all. What put you on to him?'

'You did, you and the doctor. You were talking while you waited down here, and I was on the stairs, listening. And there were three things you said that stuck in my mind like burrs, and I couldn't get rid of them. You were agreeing that Richard hadn't been robbed, because everything in his room was just as we should have expected to find it. And then Trevor said: "But shouldn't there have been something *un*expected in his room? Whatever it was Antonia gave him to remember her by." And the second thing was when Dr Randall said of course it was nonsense looking for other motives, because a motive as strong as that will couldn't exist side by side with another utterly different one. And I started thinking, no, not by accident, but could it be by design? Because that would be wonderful, wouldn't it, for the person who had the other, the unknown motive. And then Dr Randall said: "There's no ignoring the evidence of your own eyes," and Trevor said: "Not eyes – ears." And then I realised that we'd never actually read the provisions of the will, only heard them. Oh, we'd seen the thing itself, signature and all, it was hers, all right, it wasn't any fake. But we didn't *read* it, we had it read *to* us. So then, you see, there was only one person who *could* have been responsible.'

'You mean he made up all that rigmarole he read out to us? But why? What *was* his motive?'

'And why didn't you come down and tell us?' demanded the doctor indignantly. 'Why go and take such a risk alone?'

'Because you'd have argued, and there was no time left. All I wanted to prove my theory was the will. If it was really different from everything he'd told us, we didn't need any other proof. What motive could he possibly have had for falsifying it, except to provide as many as possible of us with that compelling motive for murdering Richard? So that when he *was* murdered we should all be looking at one another, and nobody should ever think of suspecting Neil.'

'But even if Richard did have something valuable enough to make him covet it, why kill him? That wasn't necessary.'

'No, but it made things much easier and safer, as long as somebody else was sure to get blamed for it, as he intended they should. If he'd simply stolen what he wanted there'd have been an alarm raised at once, because Richard treasured Mrs Byrne's gift, and must have looked at it often, and he'd raise hell if it went astray. But if Richard died, and *then* it vanished, who was to raise the alarm after it? No one else knew anything about it, no one even knew he had it, or rather no one knew what it was he had.'

'Then how did Everard get to know about it?' asked Trevor.

'He told me that. He didn't mind telling me things, he was sure I was never going to be able to tell anyone else. Do you remember after the crash-landing Richard wouldn't leave his briefcase behind, and Neil went back to get it for him? He said the case had fallen off the luggage rack and burst open. It was then he saw what was in it. He didn't take it, because he realised Richard would look or feel if it was safe the minute he got the case in his hands. But he wanted it. And he began to think how to get it. If Richard died he could safely take it, because no one else knew about it. And then, you see, Mrs Quayne insisted on the will being read, and he saw how he could provide everyone but himself with a motive, and himself with a beautiful smoke screen. Here we were, cut off from the world, with no possibility of the police taking charge at once, a lot of people with expectations, and a will he could manipulate to set them at one another's throats. So he did it. And when it was done he went straight upstairs and took the tablets from Dr Randall's bag, and later in the evening he used them. I think it must have been when he came down at about ten o'clock, and Dr Randall met him on the stairs. The door of the room was closed, there was no one else about. I think Neil went in to Richard then.'

'It must have amused him,' said the doctor

229

sombrely, 'to find Richard busy making a will. That was something he couldn't have counted on. It made the motive irresistibly convincing.'

'Yes, that was a gift to him. It made it easy for him to stay a while, you see, to advise, law being his profession. And if they were both bending over the table, concentrating on the will, it would be easy for him to slip the tablets into the brandy. As Laurence said, he wouldn't have to touch the glass.'

'But why destroy the will afterwards? As long as it wasn't finished it was better evidence where it was, and readable, than the way we found it,' said Trevor. 'I suppose, of course, he was trying to simulate the actions of a guilty Laurence, or for that matter you, Randall, or me. But there was no point in trying to hide what Richard had been doing, from that point of view, because McHugh already knew, and was spreading it round the bar. There was no secret about it. And from his own point of view he certainly wouldn't want it to be hidden. If he wanted to use it directly against one person by planting it in his room, why not just crumple it up and hide it there as it was? That would have been credible enough to pass muster, for a suspect in a hurry, and a much more infallible lead for our amateur detectives. Why this extra subtlety? You see how carefully he left enough to identify it for what it was. Then why make it so difficult? Why burn it at all?'

'That's been bothering me, too,' Susan owned. 'I still don't know the answer.'

'I can think of a possible one,' said Laurence. 'You know what Richard said when he heard she'd left him the money. Why did she do it, he said, she knew I didn't want it, she knew I had enough. It wasn't like her, he said. Well, it wouldn't be like Richard to rush to make a will like that, just to prevent us from ever hoping to get back what he'd said himself he didn't want. And I think – I really do think – maybe he was the only one who had a feeling something dirty was going on, and tried to scotch it. I think he began to make a will leaving Aunt Antonia's money back where he thought she ought to have left it, to her relatives – to my mother and me.'

'That was it!' Susan put down her cup with a crash. 'That would account for it. If that was what he'd written, the will would *have* to be destroyed, otherwise it would let out at least two of his suspects at once, and the whole scheme would crash. That will was a weapon *for* Neil only in the condition he finally left it in – identifiable as Richard's will, but otherwise totally illegible.'

'The experts will have ways of making out some of the words on the charred bits,' said Trevor. 'They do marvellous reconstructions these days. But one thing's bothering me. I'm willing to believe all that about McHugh's well-meant efforts – apparently quite disinterested efforts – singling out Laurence as the handy suspect, and your attitude confirming Neil in his idea of using him, but *when* did he plant the evidence in Laurence's room?'

'When Dr Randall sent him upstairs for his bag, when – when Mrs Quayne was ill.' It was Susan who flushed at that recollection now. Miranda had no qualms about the correctness of her own behaviour at all times. 'It was one of those moments that get overlooked, because when there's an empergency, and a doctor says do so-and-so, you just jump to do it. But if you'll think for a moment you'll remember that Neil did go upstairs alone, and he was positively the only person who did.'

'But to burn the will as carefully as that would take time. He was gone only a matter of seconds.'

'He'd already burned the will, in his own room, before midnight. Most of the ashtrays in the rooms, including his, as I saw tonight, are the same, those big beer ones the pubs get free from the local brewery. All he had to do was change the ashtrays over and hide the tablets somewhere in Laurence's room. He had time for that. We were occupied,' she said somewhat caustically, 'we weren't counting seconds.' She looked up suddenly at Laurence, and said directly: 'I'm sorry I gave you such a horrible time.'

He looked back at her, flushing, and said: 'It doesn't matter now.' But his eyes said: *If it hadn't been you I wouldn't have minded so much.* And hers replied clearly: *If it hadn't been you he picked on it wouldn't have made me so determined he should pay for it.*

'And it was my fault he tried to kill you,' she said, shivering. 'I told him I could clear you, you see. I needed help, and I thought I could trust him, of all people. It must have given him a terrible shock. He tried to convince me I shouldn't be believed. And the same night he tried to discredit my evidence in advance by staging a guilty suicide for you. I got you into that.'

'You got me out of it, too,' Laurence said. 'Dr Randall told me.' All that had blown over in the snowy wind. There was never going to be any need of reconciliations, and whatever there was to forgive, on either side, was forgiven long ago without any words.

'But there's still one baffling thing about all this,' said Trevor. 'Falsifying the will like that could only have provided Everard with temporary cover at best. He was taking that will back to his firm in England. As soon as it arrived there the cat would be out of the bag. The deception couldn't be maintained.'

'No,' agreed Susan, 'but you see, he wasn't going back to England, and neither was the will. He had his passport and a fair amount of money on him. From here on he was going to vanish. I don't know where to. Somewhere out of Europe. He was abandoning England, his practice, his society, and starting up again in another identity. There's no other explanation.'

They were all staring at her warily, as if they all saw the same implication, but were unwilling to be the first to mention it.

'Then this stake of his,' said the doctor at last, 'must have been something enormous, something big enough to make all that worth while.'

'Yes,' said Susan, 'it was. It was the Treplenburg-Feldstein diamonds.'

CHAPTER XVII

*How the world's joys cheat and elude us,
How empty all things are that we deem
    precious.*

Act 1

The silence, though brief, was fathoms deep; it seemed to Susan that every person in the room held his breath. Even Laurence hadn't known about this, even he was caught off balance, and his eyes shared the wonder, the incredulity, the faint, glittering hunger that stared from all the rest of them. But only for a moment, and distantly, as a child might contemplate a fairy-tale treasure, already forewarned that it would crumble into withered leaves when touched. The brilliant spark of greed faded again into the warmth of his gratitude that she and he were both alive, and diamonds wonderfully expendable, and she knew he would have thrown the Crown jewels down the mountain without a qualm to lift the shadow of harm from her.

'The Treplenburg-Feldstein diamonds!' breathed Trevor. 'Is it possible? I've been with her all these years, and I'd have sworn they were nothing but a myth. And to turn up now! My God, she could keep a secret, if this is true!'

Miranda asked huskily, as if her life depended on

235

the answer: 'You're sure, they *do* exist? Do you really *know*? Have you seen them?'

'I know, because he told me so himself. I haven't actually seen them, but I saw the case they're in, when he made me put back the will into his briefcase.'

'His briefcase?' Recollection clutched at Miranda's heart with an awful certainty. Her voice cracked, like a fourteen-year-old choirboy's in a moment of stress. 'But the briefcase – you said you threw it— Oh, *no*! You've thrown away the diamonds! *My* diamonds! How *could* you? Suppose they're never found again?' She jumped to her feet in a frenzy of agitation, but Laurence took her firmly by the arm and pulled her down again.

'Mother,' he said, jutting his chin with a new authority, 'be quiet! They're not yours, they never were yours, and they never will be. Aunt Antonia gave them to Richard. And if they hadn't gone over the edge I should have done, with a bullet or two in me for good measure. So think of that and shut up, unless you want us to think you'd have preferred things that way.'

'There was no mention of diamonds in the will, in any case,' said Susan consolingly. 'That's one of the things he didn't have to alter. If they do turn up again I suppose they'll go with Richard's estate.' As a generous gesture to Miranda she added: 'You won't have to worry, though, if we do recover the briefcase, because the will's there, too, and she's left you well provided for.'

They had forgotten until then that she had read the will, and knew what its true provisions were. They began to ply her with questions now; she even

236

saw in their faces the old jealous eagerness.

'He didn't have to improvise so very much, you know. All the minor things at the beginning were true. And me, that was true, she left me a hundred pounds. When it came to you it was more complicated. She linked Trevor and Dr Randall together, and left them five thousand pounds each. She called them "my very dear and very contentious friends of many years". And besides the money she left some personal things, one of her portraits to Trevor, and the eighteenth-century toy organ – she said you played it beautifully on champagne, Trevor, but best of all on Gewürztraminer – and to Dr Randall the Dresden candlesticks and the Epstein bust. And then she said you could choose whatever you thought reasonable from among her books and records, and your choice was to be undirected and unrestricted except by each other, because that was the only way you would ever be able to settle anything without fighting.'

Trevor uttered a snort of laughter. The doctor asked in a gentle, anxious voice: 'You're sure of this, Susan? You're not making it up?'

'Of course not! Those aren't all the exact words, but that was the gist of it. I couldn't forget, because it was like having her back. On one of her good days, still with that sharp flavour she had, but in a good humour—'

Dr Randall got up abruptly. 'I must go and see if my patient is sleeping,' he said, and hastily left the room.

'Oh, dear,' said Susan, dismayed, 'now I've upset him.'

'No, you haven't,' said Trevor. 'He's all right, leave

him alone. You said yourself it was like having her
back. Go on!'

'Then there was Richard. She didn't leave him any
money, just all the rest of her books and records, and
her manuscripts and letters, and the Mozart spinet,
and some personal things like that.'

She broke off, unsure of her voice. The thought
of Richard had suddenly come back to her with
terrible poignancy, so lonely and so old and so
bewildered; and it seemed to her that killing him had
been a lesser crime than depriving him of his sure
knowledge of Antonia, and his security in remembering her. She was suddenly immensely grateful to
Laurence for the few awkward words which at least
had done something to illuminate the old man's last
night in the world.

'Yes? And the rest?' prompted Miranda nervously
licking her dry lips.

'She left you an annuity for life, but I can't
remember how much it was.' She really couldn't, she
wasn't being mischievous. 'I know it seemed to me
a lot of money, I'm sure it will turn out to be
generous,' she said reassuringly. 'And the residue is
left to Laurence.' This she remembered almost word
for word. ' "To my dear nephew," she said, "the
best and most unassuming accompanist I ever had,
who fondly imagines I don't realise how carefully
and lovingly he has been nursing my failing powers
for three years, and what an effort it has sometimes
cost him to refrain from telling me to admit my age
and stop making an obstinate old fool of myself."
And then she said he was to spend lavishly while he
was young, and she hoped the first thing he'd buy
would be a horn. But she made a condition, too—'

She had gone on talking because Laurence, taken utterly by surprise, was half laughing and quite on the verge of tears, and she had to give him time to recover his breath and his balance; but now she saw to what a crisis her rush of words had brought them all, and stopped guiltily.

'Well, I'm damned!' said Laurence shakily. 'The lovely, wicked old devil, she never missed a trick.'

'A condition?' said Miranda sharply. 'What condition?'

There was no help for it, it had to come out sooner or later. Susan fixed her eyes on the whitening daylight that fingered the misted windows, and said in a small voice: 'That he lives apart from you.'

Miranda came to her feet with a rigid dignity that made her look twice her normal height. 'That is the kind of insidious attack I might have expected from Aunt Antonia.' She glared murderously at Trevor, who had considerately translated a splutter of laughter into a convulsive sneeze. 'I hope I am capable of assessing the eccentricities of an old woman at their true value. I shall not allow myself to be upset by them.' For that amount of money she would have swallowed worse affronts than this, no one doubted it.

'In any case,' said Laurence in a loud, firm voice, blushing to the ears, 'I shall be needing a separate establishment, Mother, because I'm thinking of getting married.' His eyes, bright with hope and apprehension, caught Susan's, and firmly held them. 'If she'll have me,' he said with a slightly tremulous smile.

If she'd have him! A sweet, hare-brained fool who got out of a sickbed and went crashing down a mountain in the dark and the snow to rescue a girl, without a weapon, without adequate means of helping either himself or her, without the slightest hope of success against a man with a gun. Absolutely irresponsible, except that he got there before anyone else. Totally ineffective, except that he brought her back with him. What more could she possibly want? She shut her eyes quickly, to keep from crying, and heard Miranda say in a faint, dismayed voice: 'Married?'

'And I *am* going to buy a horn,' said Laurence wildly, 'and I'm never going to touch the piano again.' It wasn't the thought of the money that was making him drunk, it was the nudge in the ribs from Antonia's ghostly elbow, the sharp old voice egging him on to shed his jesses and take flight for freedom. 'I hate pianos! As far as I'm concerned, keyboard instruments stopped with the harpsichord.'

If her eyes had not been tightly closed, and all her senses concentrated in her hearing, Susan would not have caught the knocking sounds from outside the house for the noise he was making. Curious, steady, measured raps, which by some process of divination she identified as the sound of boot-heels being drummed against the wall to dislodge accumulated growths of hard snow.

'Hush!' she said, trembling.

Laurence fell instantly silent. They all reared their heads, listening wide-eyed.

'I heard someone outside. It's them. They're coming back.'

Then they all heard the low voices and the movements of many men, going heavily and wearily. The doctor came in, and on the opening of the door the sounds were enlarged, moving in upon them.

'They're here. I saw Herr Klostermann pass the window.'

'Is he— Did they find him?' asked Laurence from a dry throat.

'I don't know. They haven't come in yet.'

Trevor crossed to the window, rubbing at the steamy pane. They came to his shoulders, peering out into the murk of the early daylight, which showed them little enough until the doctor snapped out the lights in the room. Then they could discern the big, muffled shapes of men approaching the yard gate, in a tight, steadily moving group; and in a moment they saw the reason for this close formation. They were carrying something between them on a stretcher.

Someone had run ahead to open the gate, and the bearers were halted for a moment while it was swung back to let them in. The long shape on the stretcher was draped with coats. A gloved hand, the fingers stiffly curled, jutted from the folds. The face was covered.

'He's dead,' said Susan.

Relief and regret and pity and sadness tore at her like contending winds, shaking her into uncontrollable tears. Laurence put his arms round her and drew her gently away from the window. He was astonished and moved to find that his movements had authority with her; she went gladly, and clung to him gratefully.

'It's better that way, what was there left for him now? Oh, darling, don't!' He felt her trembling, and held her the closer. 'Don't think of it any more, it's over. We couldn't have done anything for him, even if he'd come back alive. Oh, darling, don't, don't cry, it's all over now.'

But it was not quite over. Tired, deep voices filled the hall. Klostermann came in slowly, grey with fatigue, his cap in his hand. Under his arm was a black briefcase, filmed over with rime and glistening wetly now in the warmth withindoors. He laid it on the table, and chafed his cold fingers until he could unbuckle the straps. They drew into a fascinated circle round him, staring at the case that held a quarter of a million pounds' worth of diamonds and a legendary love affair.

Trevor mustered enough of his hesitant German to ask questions. They heard Neil Everard's name pass.

'How was it?' asked Laurence round the constriction of excitement and sadness in his throat. 'Did he smash himself up?'

Trevor shook his head. 'No major injuries, only battered and bruised. He froze to death. They didn't find him until it began to get light. Seems they didn't have to look for his briefcase, he'd found it. He was lying over it when they got to him.'

Klostermann had the briefcase open now. He drew out the envelope that held Antonia's will, and then a big oblong case of worn leather that had occupied most of the available space. The dark red lid was tooled in gilt with an elaborate coat of arms, the quarterings of which were so rubbed that they could not easily distinguish them, though the two supporters seemed to be blackamoor pages in turbans with tall aigrettes, one balancing a tray, the other flourishing a handkerchief. Everyone stood silent, staring intently, waiting for the case to be opened. When Klostermann lifted the lid the glitter seemed

to them blinding, because they were waiting to be
blinded.

Trevor said in a queer, still voice: 'Oh, my good God
almighty!'

'Kennen Sie diese Juwelen?'

There was a deep collar of brilliants, a flexible
tiara, a pair of clasps in the form of a double eagle,
two bracelets and a great pendant. They blazed out
of the bed of black velvet with a deceptive
splendour, and then, crystallising into things truly
seen instead of more than half imagined, became
what they were, adornments for a stage costume,
tinsel beautifully made, with love and artistry, but
tinsel.

'Know them? Yes, I know them. I haven't seen
them since she left the operatic stage, but I know
them all right. So he killed for these! Threw away
his career and everything he had and was – for
these!'

Trevor turned abruptly, and crossed the room to
rummage hastily through the pile of papers on a side
table, and came back with the magazine he had
bought at Schwechat before they boarded the plane.
He held out to them the picture of Antonia and
Richard in *Rosenkavalier*. There was the turret of
brilliants in the powdered hair, the glittering collar
about her throat, the bracelets on her wrists, the
double eagle in the foam of lace at her breast.

'Treplenburg-Feldstein diamonds, my foot! I never
did believe in them. It was only a glimpse of the case
that first tempted him, of course, and I suppose those
armorial bearings have a convincingly archducal
look, unless you're in on the joke. If he did risk a look
inside it was only one glance by torchlight, they'd

more than stand up to that. But if he went on believing in them to the end – and poor devil, I rather hope he did! – his specialist knowledge evidently didn't extend to opera or diamonds. *That* is an imaginative craftsman's idea of the coat of arms of the Princess von Werdenberg. *Those* are the stage regalia the Salzburg company had made as a present for Antonia, when she sang the Marschallin for the hundredth time. She never sang it again without them, they were her good-luck charm.'

They stood in dead silence, staring at the brittle stones for which two people had died, and two more gone very near to death.

'Do you mean to say,' whispered Susan, clinging with cold hands to Laurence's arm, 'that all this was for nothing? He killed Richard and destroyed himself for *nothing*?'

'Oh, I wouldn't say nothing. If values really exist in the mind I suppose he died with a quarter of a million in his arms. To Richard these things were beyond price. And even for what they are, they have a certain value. They're good paste,' said Trevor ironically, 'and excellent workmanship. I shouldn't be surprised if they're worth every penny of a hundred pounds!'

EDITH PARGETER

SHE GOES TO WAR

It is 1940. Catherine Saxon is on her way to join the
Women's Royal Naval Service at its Quarters in
Devonport. She isn't quite sure why she joined up in
the first place. A journalist on a local paper, her brief
had been to cover gossip and fashion, so she was
hardly in the front line! But join up she did, and her
impulsive decision is to have undreamt-of
consequences . . .

Sent first for basic training as a teleprinter operator,
Catherine is surprised to find she enjoys the
camaraderie of her fellow Wrens and quickly grows
to love the beautiful Devon countryside. A posting to
Liverpool comes as something of a shock, but she
soon acclimatises to the war-torn city, and it is here,
one fine day in early spring, that she meets the man
who is to have such a profound effect on her life.

Tom Lyddon is a veteran of the Spanish Civil War
and his political beliefs strike an immediate chord
with Catherine. In wartime, the usual stages of
courtship are dispensed with, and she readily accepts
Tom's invitation to spend a few days with him in the
blissful solitude of the North Wales countryside.
Their idyll ends when Tom is recalled to active
service abroad, and then all Catherine can do is wait
– and hope – for her lover's safe return . . .

FICTION / GENERAL 0 7472 3277 6

A Rare Benedictine

The Advent of Brother Cadfael

Ellis Peters

'Brother Cadfael sprang to life suddenly and unexpectedly when he was already approaching sixty, mature, experienced, fully armed and seventeen years tonsured.' So writes Ellis Peters in her introduction to *A Rare Benedictine* – three vintage tales of intrigue and treachery, featuring the monastic sleuth who has become such a cult figure of crime fiction. The story of Cadfael's entry into the monastery at Shrewsbury has been known hitherto only to a few readers; now his myriad fans can discover the chain of events that led him into the Benedictine Order.

Lavishly adorned with Clifford Harper's beautiful illustrations, these three tales show Cadfael at the height of his sleuthing form, with all the complexities of plot, vividly evoked Shropshire backgrounds and warm understanding of the frailties of human nature that have made Ellis Peters an international bestseller.

'A must for Cadfael enthusiasts – quite magical' *Best*
'A beautifully illustrated gift book' *Daily Express*
'A book for all Cadfael fans to treasure' *Good Book Guide*
'Brother Cadfael has made Ellis Peters' historical whodunnits a cult series' *Daily Mail*

HISTORICAL FICTION / CRIME 0 7472 3420 5

More Compelling Fiction from Headline Review

BY FIRELIGHT

A CLASSIC NOVEL FROM THE MASTER STORYTELLER

Edith Pargeter

Moving, intriguing and beautifully written, BY FIRELIGHT is a classic novel from the oeuvre of Edith Pargeter.

The untimely death of Claire Falchion's husband leaves her feeling numb, as if a phase has ended but not as if any great change has occurred. Her friend Leonora says that Claire cannot complain; she'd had everything for as long as she could expect – a career as a novelist, a husband and a child. But there is nothing within Claire except an emptiness.

She retreats to a dilapidated old schoolhouse in the tranquil village of Sunderne. But her peace is threatened by the quiet presence of her neighbour, Jonathan Kenton, with whom an acquaintance is growing, despite Claire's attempts to resist it. And the house itself seems to be unleashing strange ideas that Claire cannot explain, almost like having second sight. Even Claire's pen seems to be writing of its own accord – memories of a witch hunt in Sunderne appear on the page and the terrible scenes come alive in the countryside around her: scenes of a trial, of superstitions, of lies and pain, that end with a cruel burning.

FICTION / GENERAL 0 7472 4561 4

A selection of bestsellers from Headline

APPOINTED TO DIE	Kate Charles	£4.99	☐
SIX FOOT UNDER	Katherine John	£4.99	☐
TAKEOUT DOUBLE	Susan Moody	£4.99	☐
POISON FOR THE PRINCE	Elizabeth Eyre	£4.99	☐
THE HORSE YOU CAME IN ON	Martina Grimes	£5.99	☐
DEADLY ADMIRER	Christine Green	£4.99	☐
A SUDDEN FEARFUL DEATH	Anne Perry	£5.99	☐
THE ASSASSIN IN THE GREENWOOD	P C Doherty	£4.99	☐
KATWALK	Karen Kijewski	£4.50	☐
THE ENVY OF THE STRANGER	Caroline Graham	£4.99	☐
WHERE OLD BONES LIE	Ann Granger	£4.99	☐
BONE IDLE	Staynes & Storey	£4.99	☐
MISSING PERSON	Frances Ferguson	£4.99	☐

All Headline books are available at your local bookshop or newsagent, or can be ordered direct from the publisher. Just tick the titles you want and fill in the form below. Prices and availability subject to change without notice.

Headline Book Publishing, Cash Sales Department, Bookpoint, 39 Milton Park, Abingdon, OXON, OX14 4TD, UK. If you have a credit card you may order by telephone – 01235 400400.

Please enclose a cheque or postal order made payable to Bookpoint Ltd to the value of the cover price and allow the following for postage and packing:

UK & BFPO: £1.00 for the first book, 50p for the second book and 30p for each additional book ordered up to a maximum charge of £3.00.
OVERSEAS & EIRE: £2.00 for the first book, £1.00 for the second book and 50p for each additional book.

Name ....

Address ....

....

....

If you would prefer to pay by credit card, please complete:
Please debit my Visa/Access/Diner's Card/American Express (delete as applicable) card no:

Signature .... Expiry Date ....